THE House ON THE CORNER

KAREN EDWARDS COOK

THE House ON THE CORNER

XULON PRESS

Xulon Press
555 Winderley Pl, Suite 225
Maitland, FL 32751
407.339.4217
www.xulonpress.com

© 2024 by Karen Edwards Cook

All rights reserved solely by the author. The author guarantees all contents are original and do not infringe upon the legal rights of any other person or work. No part of this book may be reproduced in any form without the permission of the author.

Due to the changing nature of the Internet, if there are any web addresses, links, or URLs included in this manuscript, these may have been altered and may no longer be accessible. The views and opinions shared in this book belong solely to the author and do not necessarily reflect those of the publisher. The publisher therefore disclaims responsibility for the views or opinions expressed within the work.

Paperback ISBN-13: 978-1-66289-199-1
eBook ISBN-13: 978-1-66289-200-4

Dedication

I dedicate this book to the my Mother, Leah Singrey-Edwards who instilled the love of books in me and my English Literature teacher, Sally Hagerty, who told me, "Some day Karen, you will write a book and people will buy it."

Table of Contents

Dedication..vii

Chapter 1	The Move	1
Chapter 2	More Surprises	5
Chapter 3	Noises	10
Chapter 4	The Office Comes Together	14
Chapter 5	Unwanted Visitor	19
Chapter 6	Visit to Dr. Lajonque	23
Chapter 7	Unscheduled Meeting	28
Chapter 8	Research Time	30
Chapter 9	College Visit	34
Chapter 10	Unknown Caller	73
Chapter 11	More Investigation	92
Chapter 12	The Meeting	101
Chapter 13	The Hospital	145

THE House ON THE CORNER

Chapter 14 Nursing Care	169
Chapter 15 Road Trip	177
Chapter 16 Farm Visit	180
Chapter 17	210
Chapter 18	212
Epilogue	215

CHAPTER 1

the Move

Mercedes Adler was a country girl, born and raised, but every time she brought the girls to see Dr. Lajonque in the nearby town of Pedeuax, she felt an attraction to the small city lifestyle she couldn't explain. At home on the farm, there was always something to do, always another chore calling her away from her writing; Mercedes began to think a small house in town might serve her needs better.

She was looking for a house in town, in a location where she could study people and get ideas for her characters in her books. Her realtor said there was listing for a house that was built in 1845. Once she saw this house, she fell in love with it. The second floor had been converted into an apartment but was no longer being used. The doors had been removed by some thieves looking to sell the metal. Whatever furniture had been in the rooms appeared to have been stolen as none was there.

THE *House* ON THE CORNER

She decided to take a long look at the basement. She wanted to see if she could put shelves down there to store her books as well as make a place where she could research certain items without being interrupted. She opened the only door the thieves hadn't taken and turned on the light switch near the door. As the 25-watt bulb cast a dim cone of light, she could just about see the steps. Walking down the steps, they felt somewhat slippery—not too slippery, just a little bit—like someone was carrying a bucket of water and some of it had splashed out. She thought, *I should have brought a flashlight. Must put this on my list of things to buy for the house.* About the time she got to the bottom step, something ran across her foot. She jumped and peered into the darkness to get an idea of what it was. Unable to discern what it was, she continued down the steps into the basement, and as she took the next step, her foot hit something solid. She turned and ran back up the stairs to look for a candle, a match, a cigarette lighter, or anything she could use to try to see what she'd just kicked with her foot.

Since she'd quit smoking, there was no cigarette lighter in her pocket. *Think,* she told myself, *think. Now where is the box with the candles for my first night here?* Moving through the kitchen, into the pantry, she spotted the shoebox marked "candles" and pulled out two long tapered candles. *Thank God.* There were matches under the candles.

The Move

Lighting one candle and putting the other unlit one in my pocket, she headed for the basement. As she began slowly moving down the steps, the doorbell rang. *What an awful ring. Sounds like something from an old Vincent Price movie.* The sound was "go-onng, go-onng, go-onng." She went back upstairs, snuffed the candle, and opened the door. Lying on the doorstep facing her was a package addressed to "Sophie's Silkys." The return address simply stated, "Sophie's Friend."

Okay, one of my friends has decided to send a gag housewarming gift. Little did they know that Sophie (her silky terrier who was presently being boarded at the vet's) was not there, nor were her sisters Sadie and Daisy.

She was nowhere ready for the girls to come home. *Enough,* she told myself, and she brought the package into the kitchen, placed it on the counter, and headed back down to the basement. At the end of the steps, she lit the candle and again peered into the darkness. Looking down at the floor, she saw a tarp covering something long, horizontal shaped. Very gingerly, she moved the tarp and gasped; there was a skeleton under it! Judging by the bone size, it may have been a full-grown dog, and the dog had been dead for a long time. The collar was leather, somewhat dry rotted, but one could make out a few of the numbers and letters: "100 W. Main, Bcgcrt."

THE *House* ON THE CORNER

She wondered how long it had been there. The real estate agent told her the house had been used for other things. It had been an office for a finance company and a yarn store, and the upstairs had been a secondhand store and most recently an apartment. She said that it was only a few years ago those people had moved out. *Must check with her to see how long it has been since the basement apartments were used.*

Looking further into the shadows, she saw that all the doors down there had also been removed, as well as most of the walls, making the basement one very large room. It would be easy to make bookshelves. She saw two dog dishes over in a corner. She went over and picked up one of the dishes to inspect it. As she turned it over, she saw the same numbers and letters from the leather collar stamped on the dish. This time the word in front was "Bogart." The other dish was stamped "Airedale Rescuers, April, 1847."

CHAPTER 2

More Surprises

I went back over to the skeleton of the dog. I thought to myself, *This must be an Airedale, but surely it hasn't been here since 1847?* It made no sense that this skeleton of a dog was there. There'd been no one living or working in this house for several years. *That's it,* I told myself, *someone has brought the skeleton of the dog and dumped it in my basement. I bet the person who did this was trying to scare me or play a very cruel joke.* Looking around again, I decided it was likely a mouse that ran across my foot. *Better put mouse traps on the list as well.*

Okay, now I've got to get the skeleton of the dog out of the basement. As I headed outside to go to the garage for an oversized garbage bag, something caught my eye. There, hanging on the door handle of the summer kitchen, was a grocery bag. Inside the bag was another box with a card attached with writing in black and white print. I opened the card, and inside was a very old picture of an Airedale dog. The dog was hanging by its back legs from a tree limb. I stared at the note, not comprehending the meaning. The note only said, "Your dogs could end up like this." *Is someone trying to scare me? Does someone not want me to live here, or is someone trying to warn me?*

I went back into the house and headed up the steps to the second floor, and I was pleased with the way it has been kept. All the walls were painted white, and there were no picture holes in them. One bedroom had a fireplace on one side, but part of the mantle was missing. There was a window seat with torn pillows lying across the seat. One strip of fabric was saturated with a red stain.

I picked up the pillow and held it under my nose. *It smells of wine.* The smell wasn't as old as the pillow, which told me someone may have broken the locks on the doors and had been upstairs drinking. *Hope they had a good time as they won't be back.*

I made another mental note to myself: *Call security company first thing in the morning.* In the other bedroom, someone had left an old iron bed. *The mattress is stained; vagrants must have found their way in. Lots of trash to move out. It will take a long to get this place the way that I want it.*

More Surprises

Going into the bathroom, I found the clawfoot tub looked really good. Someone had even taken the time to paint the toenails of the claws black. *Hmm. They left the brass fixtures on the sink and the tub.* The window to the bathroom was covered in some sort of iron mesh.

Another mental note: *Take the iron mesh off the window.* As I tried to look through the mesh, I heard a noise. It was a low, guttural sound, close to where I was standing. I slowly turned around, and . . . there was nothing there. *Okay, okay, my mind must be playing tricks on me.* I went back downstairs and started bringing in things from my truck. I had to get my sleeping bag as well as blankets and pillows. The movers wouldn't be there until the afternoon of the next day, and I wanted to make sure I had the house halfway up to speed so they would have a nice, clean place to put my furniture. As I went out to the truck, it occurred to me there was an outside entrance to the basement, like the old stable doors you see in books. I noticed there was a large combination lock keeping intruders from getting in. The sun was starting to fade, so I hurried to get my sleeping bag, pillows, and makeup case that was holding shampoo, soap, toothpaste, a toothbrush, and other essentials. I remembered to pick up towels and wash cloths. I wanted to take a shower and put on my new jammies—might as well enjoy the feel of new jammies. After all,

THE House ON THE CORNER

I was moving into a new house. I picked up my gym bag with my clothes in it for the next day. *Now I'm set.*

Just as I started toward the sidewalk to go to my front door, a man came around the corner. He was dirty, and even at a distance, he was smelly. His hair was matted, and his face was filthy. He stopped, looked at me, squinted his eyes, and grinned, showing dirty teeth that were yellow with tobacco stain. Every other tooth was missing, and his breath was rancid. I started to back away as I began to become ill.

"What's yer name, pretty lady? From 'roun' here, or are you from the city? Movin' in here, are ya? If so, I'm a pretty good handyman. Can fix anything that needs fixing. Don't charge much either. Jus' enough to get me sumpin' to eat and a little drink once in a while," Mr. Putridbreath stated. He then took one of his grubby fingers and started to reach out to touch my hair. I jerked back. He opened his mouth and let out a loud laugh the people on the next block could hear. Suddenly, a car pulled up.

The men in it opened the doors. Mr. Putridbreath saw this and took off down the street. As I turned to look at the men in the car, the car pulled off, peeling rubber. Shouts were coming from the car; they were all swearing, calling names, and threatening physical harm to Mr. Putridbreath. As the scene unfolded before my eyes, Mr. Putridbreath suddenly disappeared. Just like that, he vanished into thin air. *What is going on around here?* As I went back into the house, I saw a car across the street in the church parking lot. Inside was a person who appeared to be waiting for someone.

Oh, well, I hope they aren't in a hurry, as no one seems to be around here.

Back in the house, I finished putting some of the bathroom essentials away. I did have the presence of mind to bring toilet tissue, soap, towels, and washcloths and a variety of personal hygiene products.

Suddenly, the day caught up with me. I was very tired and could hardly keep my eyes open, so like my mom always said, "If you get this tired, you need to go to bed." Well, she didn't have to tell me twice. I changed into my jammies, made the bed with my new Ralph Lauren sheets and blanket, got my favorite pillows and tossed them on the bed, put my fuzzy house slippers next to the bed, took the portable radio from the gym bag and put it on top of the dresser, and plugged in my cell phone and put it next to my sleeping bag. I didn't even remember falling asleep.

CHAPTER 3

Noises

Noise, noise, noise . . . where is this coming from? I was disoriented, and my sleeping bag was moving; someone or something was pushing it. "Help!" I called out, but no one came to help me. I still couldn't make out what was going on.

Around and around and around I go. Where I'll stop, I don't know. A bright light was shining in my eyes.

"It hurts; make it stop. Please, make it stop!"

My head was hurting, I couldn't open my eyes—the light was still there. I was tied up into a ball and couldn't move my hands. I tried to feel my clothes, but nothing was there, only my flesh. *Where are my clothes?* I remembered putting on my pajamas. *Where are my pajamas?*

I couldn't open my mouth; my tongue wouldn't move. I was cold, very cold. I pushed against something hard. It felt like a board. No, not a board; cement. It was very cold.

Where am I? I summoned all the strength one person could possibly muster. I pushed as hard as my body would allow and freed one my hands. As I touched the cement, it started to crumble. I was rolling…rolling around and around like a top off its axis, and then I felt myself falling. My arm was outstretched; I wanted to catch myself as my hand hit something hard. The bright light was gone.

I opened my eyes. I was in my bedroom, in my sleeping bag with my pajamas on. No sign of my sleeping bag being moved or anything else.

I reached over for my cell phone, picked it up. *What?* It was the next day. It was 8:00 in the morning.

"Oh, my God!" I yelled. I was supposed to meet the movers at 7:30. Good thing they were late. I hurried and got dressed, pulling on clothes faster than a fireman going to a fire.

You know how it feels when you have a dream that is "too real?" Well, that's the way I felt that day. I was sure the dream I had the night before meant something, but I didn't know what. I guessed I would find out when the time was right.

The movers finally arrived, only two hours late. It seemed that coming from a major city to a small town without the aid of a GPS was not easy for city people, especially when they had to stop the local folk to ask for directions.

THE *House* ON THE CORNER

As the movers unloaded and placed my furniture where I wanted it, I saw the same car in the parking lot of the church again. As with the day before, there was someone inside the car. I made a mental note to go over and ask what the deal was if they were still there by the time the movers left. I wondered whom they were watching and why.

I used my cell phone to call the local internet company; I needed to get wireless access for my computer. There were a lot of books to unpack, but first I needed to get the shelves secured as well as get the dog skeleton out of the basement. I thought that maybe the internet people might know someone who wanted to make some extra money and would be willing to build the shelves for me as well as lay some tile down in order to absorb some of the noise. I hoped that this person might also know a little about putting in something that would keep my books from gathering any type of mold by being in the basement.

Even though the books weren't necessarily first editions, some were quite old, and I knew that at an auction, if the right people were there, they would fetch a pretty penny.

The internet people arrived. I was only expecting one person, but three technicians came; two were apprentices who are learning the trade.

The name of the internet company was "Greene Aces Internet Experts." Their mission statement spoke of setting up your computer so no air waves were compromised, nor were any ozone issues created.

I wasn't too worried about this; I just wanted my computer up and running. I relied on my computer to keep track of my books. They were cataloged on my computer as well as several memory sticks. It took the tech squad all day to get things connected. We agreed to go with wireless connections as the walls were cement, and it would cost a small fortune to connect that way.

CHAPTER 4

The Office Comes Together

After the internet technicians left, I started unpacking more boxes and moving some of the furniture in order to create a "space" for my writing. I decided to use the front room of the house for my office and writing.

Being an older house, it was sited so the morning sun came in the northeast windows and the afternoon sun came in the west windows. All that natural light saved on electricity.

I looked out the window, and the car at the church was gone, but another one had replaced it. I couldn't tell if someone is in it or if the people were parked there so they could go to a restaurant down the street. I put them out of my mind and continued working on the house.

The day started to turn into night, and I was tired. I realized I hadn't eaten all day, so I went upstairs to get a quick shower and put on some clean clothes. The shower felt good as the warm water ran down my aching back.

Once clean, I dried off and put on my navy turtleneck, clean jeans, funky doggie socks (all my socks have dog prints on them), and black half-boots. I found those boots in a thrift store. They were Italian and must have cost a pretty penny new. I only paid $4.00 for them, and they were the most comfortable shoes I'd owned for a long time.

I grabbed my navy corduroy jacket and headed down the street to a bistro that served Italian food. I'd heard one of the internet guys talking about how good the pasta was and thought that sounded good.

As I walked into the establishment, I saw a young man sitting at the bar. He was blond, somewhat good looking, staring sullenly at the drink in front of him. His cell phone was lying on the bar near his drink.

He turns as I walked behind him to the restaurant. I could see him in my peripheral vision. After I was seated, I perused the menu and settled on a salad and spaghetti. Nothing too exciting; I didn't want something that would make me feel stuffed all night. I ordered an iced tea to drink. I always carried a notepad with me and pulled it out of my purse to make my list for the next day. As I was writing, the young man with blond hair walked over to my table.

THE *House* ON THE CORNER

"Good evening, miss. My name is Al Pedosta. Are you visiting, or did you just move here?" he asked. I looked at him and said, "I don't want to be rude, Mr. Pedosta. However, I'm very tired and trying to enjoy my meal; if you don't mind, I would just like to be alone."

"Listen, lady, I don't usually walk up to strange women and start a conversation, but I want to let you know if you are the person who bought the house down the street on the corner, you should know there is a lot of history that goes with that house, and I'm sure the good realtor didn't make it a point to tell you about it," he said with conviction.

I had a way of looking at a person and letting them know I didn't really care what they thought, but my curiosity got the better of me. "Okay," I said, "I'll play your silly game. Yes, I did buy the house on the corner, but contrary to what you might think, the realtor did try very hard to dissuade me from buying it because of what he called 'a past that was less than desirable.'" I continued, "Being the person I am, the corner house was exactly what I've been looking for for a long time, and I fell in love with it the first time I looked at it. Just what is your interest in this?"

He started to sit down, and he looked out the window and saw something or someone that disturbed him. Without a word, he turned, hurried out the door, turned left toward the movie theatre, and disappeared.

When the waiter came with my iced tea, I asked him if he knew the young blond man who was just at my table. He looked blankly at me and shook his head no.

God, this day just keeps getting better! Thank God the movers placed the furniture where I directed and I had an actual bed to sleep in. The next day I had to get the rest of the supplies, then come back and start trying to find someone to lay the tile in the basement and build the bookshelves.

After dinner, the evening became uneventful. I watched a little television, got bored with it, and decided to go to bed.

As I changed into my pajamas, a noise that sounded like a "thud" caught my attention. The house was dark as the lights were turned out with the exception of the bedroom light. Gingerly, I opened the bedside table drawer, took out a flashlight, and turned it on. Walking slowly to the light switch, being careful not to bump into anything, I turned the light on. Something brushed the top of my head with a "swoosh." I jumped about five feet, swung the flashlight in the direction I thought whatever hit my head went, and saw two red eyes staring back at me from the corner of the ceiling.

I ran screaming down the stairs, feeling for my cell phone. My hands were shaking. My breath was coming in small, quick gasps. I was afraid I would go into a panic attack. I kept feeling for the cell and finally found it in the bottom of my jeans pocket. Pulling it out, I started punching the buttons for 9-1-1, but whatever was in the corner stirred and flew directly for my head.

As I ducked through the basement door, the intruder flew past my head at warp speed and crashed into the basement wall.

CHAPTER 5

Unwanted Visitor

Gathering my breath, I pulled myself together and called 9-1-1. The operator answered, "9-1-1, what is your emergency?" I tried to explain what had just happened and how the intruder was lying stunned on my basement floor. The person answering the phone assured me that it was most likely a bat and this was not considered a life-threatening emergency. However, she would make the nuisance control officer aware of my situation, and he would arrive as soon as possible to remove the bat. "Okay," I told myself, "this is going to be all right." The people would come to remove the bat or whatever it was, and I would be able to go to bed and get some sleep. I walked up the steps to the kitchen and heard noises outside.

Walking into the front living room, I moved the curtains aside and saw some people standing on the corner. The street light cast a dim glow on them. They appeared to be talking to each other and pointing toward my house. One of them must have had the feeling someone was looking at him, and he turned and sees me. He was the blond-haired man, Al Pedosta. The look on his face told me he wasn't engaged in a pleasant conversation. He then said something to the other people, and they all left the area, each of them heading in opposite directions.

Now, what was that about? Don't know, don't care. I was tired and wanted to go to bed and get a good night's sleep. *I'll try to find out more tomorrow when it's daylight. I'll be able to think better when I'm not tired.*

The rest of the night was uneventful. The next thing I knew, the alarm clock on the radio was blaring. I turned over, turned it off, swung my legs over the bed, stood up, and stretched. Time for a few exercises.

As I moved toward the window seat, I noticed a car in the church parking lot across the street. I'd seen this car before, but I couldn't remember where. It was a dark-colored car, something foreign made. I couldn't tell what the make and model was, but it appeared to be empty. Maybe it was someone going to early Mass. Who knew?

Oh, well, guess I'd better get ready for the day. I took a shower, fixed my hair, put on just a dab of makeup, and head down the stairs to the kitchen. I put on the coffee, fixed

Unwanted Visitor

some toast, and sat down at the breakfast bar. Then I heard a knock on the door. A young man was standing there holding newspapers.

"Did you just move in here? If so, I'm Cory, the newspaper boy. I can make you a good deal on the morning paper. Subscribe for two months, get one month free. Then at the end of the third month, if you like the paper, you can sign up for the rest of the year at the regular price. What do you think?" he asked.

"Okay, Cory, you're quite the salesman. I'll take your special." I got my checkbook and wrote Cory a check, and he handed me the paper. With a big grin, he said, "Thank you, miss. See you tomorrow."

I got back to my stool, sat down, and started reading the paper. On the front page was a picture of Al Pedosta, the young man I had seen the day before. The headline read, "Murder Hits Pedeaux." The story below it read:

> Al Pedosta, longtime advocate for the homeless, was found stabbed in a car behind an abandoned house on Mulberry Street. Detectives state Mr. Pedosta's wallet was intact. No money or credit cards were missing. It is unknown why Mr. Pedosta was in the area where he was found. However, detectives revealed Mr. Pedosta was stabbed several times.

THE *House* ON THE CORNER

Further details will be forthcoming as the investigation continues.

Pedosta, Pedosta, why is that name so familiar? I'd heard it or read about the name somewhere.

Maybe I'll go on the computer and look up the name on Facebook or Myspace.

CHAPTER 6

Visit to Dr. Lajonque

Social networking had joined texting as a new fad for young people. I remembered watching two girls walking through a grocery store texting each other. How did I know they were doing this? Their mother admonished them, telling them they were sisters and could talk with each other; they didn't have to text each other.

I finished reading the paper, drank my coffee, took my morning pills, and pulled out my "list of things to do" for the day. The first place I needed to go is to the vet's office to make arrangements for the girls to stay with him for another week. This would give me more time to get the "doggy door" installed and the kennel built in the backyard. I'd known Dr. Gerald Lajonque for years, having worked with him on various projects when I was employed by the State of Ohio as a fraud investigator for the Department of Agriculture.

THE *House* ON THE CORNER

I decided to bring along the picture of the Airedale for Dr. Lajonque to study and give me his opinion.

Once this was taken care of, I would see the girls (so they'd know I haven't abandoned them), then go to the nearest home accessory store and purchase new locks, door fixtures, window locks, as well as various and sundry supplies needed to get started on making this house a home for me and the girls.

I got into my car and drove to Dr. Lajonque's office. As usual, it was busy, with office staff interviewing the clients' owners, distributing prescriptions, getting clients from the kennels for their anxious owners, and, judging from the noise from the back, getting out of the way for a very large dog coming through the doors.

Out came Buster, a large bull mastiff / Great Dane cross. While he had the looks of the mastiff—wide head with very big feet—he had the height of the Dane. He was beautiful, black with white paws and a white saddle pattern on his back and sides.

Buster's owner was just as gorgeous as he was. He was very tall, dark hair, crystal clear blue eyes, with a dimple on the side of his mouth. How did I know about the dimple? He looked in my direction when he came through the door and smiled.

Ah, well, no time to worry about that now, too much to do. I waited my turn and finally was able to see Dr. Lajonque. He, as usual, was just finishing cleaning up from a surgical procedure.

When he came into the office, he looked over the top of his glasses, took a deep breath, and said, "Well, Adler, here to pick up the girls? What's this I heard, you bought a house here in town? Tired of living in the country?"

"No, I would never tire of living in the country. I still have my house in the country. I got a chance to buy the house on the corner of Mulberry and Main. It is the oldest house in town, has been kept up most of the years, and I always admired it." I continued, "I need you to keep the girls for a couple of more weeks as I'm not quite ready for them, plus there's some things I found, and I need your help in figuring out what's going on. Until I figure it out, I don't want the girls in any type of danger."

Dr. Lajonque folded his arms across his chest, leaned against the examining table and with the look of a father getting ready to admonish his child, and stated, "Adler, you know as well as I do that you take things too literally. There isn't anything wrong with the house, except that it *is* old. As far as danger, you're in Pedeaux, Ohio. What can happen here? This is an old Quaker town with a small private college attended by students whose parents are either loaded, or these kids have made the kind of grades that any college in the US would be proud to have them on their campus."

I had enough Scandinavian in me with a touch of English and German to make me the stubborn person I'd grown up to be. "Okay, Dr. Lajonque, I want you to look at this photo I found in the basement along with something I have in the trunk of my Jeep. Once you've evaluated what is in the trunk, I want you to call me. Don't care what time of day or night, just want you to use your expertise to tell me what your feelings are."

Dr. Lajonque took the photo from my hand, began examining it, and stated, "All right, let's see what else you have." We walked out through the waiting area to the parking lot. I opened the trunk hatch on the Jeep and took out an old Army duffle bag. Dr. Lajonque took the bag from my hands and stated he would get back to me in a few days. He walked back into the office with me tagging behind.

Once inside, I asked Nila (the office assistant) to let Dr. Lajonque know I was going back to see the girls. If he needed me, I would be there for a while.

Sadie, Sophie, and Daisy were happy to see me. I put their harnesses on them, got their leashes, took them out of their cages, and we went out the backdoor to play in the backyard. Gosh did they have energy, running around, chasing each other, rolling in the grass, and having a wonderful time.

Visit to Dr. Lajonque

You know how you get the feeling someone is watching you? I looked over at the old car lot close to where my car was parked. To my surprise there stood two of the young men I saw talking to Al Pedosta on the corner the night before. My phone was in my side pocket, so as they started walking toward me, I held the three leashes in one hand while waiting on them to say or do something.

CHAPTER 7

Unscheduled Meeting

Sadie was the smallest of my three girls. She was also the boss of the other two. As the young men got closer, Sadie made a low growling sound, alerting Sophie and Daisy of impending danger. They stood alert, waiting on the next order from Sadie.

When the young men were about four feet from us, the shorter of the two said to the other one, "Guess Al got what was coming to him. Teach him to put his nose where it didn't belong. Hope other people will figure it out!" He then looked at me with a crooked, toothy grin.

The other one was taller and fatter. He didn't look right or left, just kept walking to the sidewalk, crossed the street, and disappeared behind the old K-Mart store.

Didn't realize until they had left how much my hands were sweating. I know my face was red, as it turns that way when I get nervous.

I let the girls play for a little while longer while watching over my shoulder. After about half an hour, I took them into the office, back to the kennels, and put them in their cage. (They had one large cage as they are small and can fit into one large cage).

Dr. Lajonque was nowhere to be found. *When did he leave, and where did he go?* I had seen him standing in the lab looking at the picture of the Airedale when I went to get the girls. *Wonder what happened. Maybe he got an emergency call. More than likely that's where he went. I'll try to call him later.* I decided to go to the library because my internet wouldn't be ready for another week, and I wanted to do some research on Al Pedosta.

CHAPTER 8

Research Time

With my laptop in hand, I walked into the library. While they didn't have a bank of computers for folks to use, they did have access to the internet via wireless connection. The librarian's name was Belinda White. She'd been the head librarian for just a few years, having been promoted when Mrs. Reed (never did know her first name) retired after forty-four years. Belinda had been with the library since she graduated from high school. She started out as a clerk, moved up to assistant librarian in about fifteen years, then received the promotion after Mrs. Reed's retirement.

After getting my access information, I went to a desk in the corner, set my computer up, and typed into the search engine, "Al Pedosta obituary." It read:

Research Time

Allen (Al) Pedosta, 24, was born on September 12, 1987 in Meridian, Ohio. Having graduated from Meridian High School where he excelled in the arts program, he continued his education at Ashball College, where he was a senior. He was scheduled for graduation in the winter quarter.

Al was preceded in death by his parents, Mary and Ed Pedosta of Pedeaux, his grandparents, and a host of friends from Ashball College. At Al's request, there will be no services. He unselfishly donated his body to Ashball College, Department of Anatomy. A special thanks to all the friends for their love and support.

The Kokely Funeral Home, Pedeaux, is honored to care for Mr. Pedosta's friends.

Wow, this is amazing. A young man gets murdered, and he made arrangements ahead of time to have his body donated to the college? This sounds like something out of an Alfred Hitchcock movie. Gives me the creeps. My curiosity got the best of me; I wanted to know just what the two young men meant with their comments this morning. They had to have known he was murdered, didn't they?

THE *House* ON THE CORNER

I continued to read the online newspaper I found the obituary in. I had a habit of looking at the classified ads, as I was always looking for something with a fox hunting theme. This could be pictures, statues, hunting clothes, hunting club meetings, statuaries, or photos.

Well, how about this. In a small ad was a note to someone. It stated, "John, the eagle has landed. Meet me at Sutters Hotel at 10:00 tonight. I'll be waiting."

Huh? Are you serious? This isn't an old movie. We are in the twenty-first century. What happened to the cell phone, or for that matter, the computer? This really is kind of "cloak and dagger."

Now, my curiosity was really piqued. Something told me I need to get a salad at Sutters Hotel that night. After all, I didn't have to go too far; it was just across the street from my new house. But first, I wanted to know where the two young men went, what they meant about Al getting what he deserved, and where Dr. Lajonque went earlier today.

If Al was a student at Ashball College, I wondered if the two young men attended that school also. *Might be a good time to take a walk around campus.* The campus was huge, and parking was difficult to find, but I could get lucky and find a place.

Yes, this was my lucky day. I found a parking place in front of the administration building. I got out of the car, locked it, and started walking. Just as I turned on the sidewalk to walk past Drake Hall, one of the dormitories, a very tall man came running from the building and ran into the street. He just missed getting hit by a UPS truck. He turned again and ran the other way. *What the heck is going on?*

Now, where was I going? It dawned on me I hadn't eaten anything since early in the morning. I decided to head over to the cafeteria. Most of the kids there would think I was a teacher, and the teachers would think I was just taking a few courses as no one knows every student in a college.

No wonder there was a parking place in front of the administration building. The walk from there to the cafeteria felt like three miles. It was hot, and I was starting to sweat. *Who does this in late summer?* Nope, I didn't like this. Give me air conditioning any time.

CHAPTER 9

Unknown Caller

Walking into the cafeteria took me back to my own college days. Lots of students were talking, and the room noise sounded like bees in a hive. Looking around, I saw the two young men I had seen at the vet clinic. I wondered what they were saying.

The shorter one saw me. He whispered to the other one, and they picked their stuff up off the table and left out a side door, which was curious.

First, though, I needed something to eat. I ordered my lunch, received it, and looked over to the table where the two boys had been sitting. There was an older man eating at the next table. He didn't seem to be paying any attention to the students or to much of anything else. He was focused on the newspaper. I saw a folded piece of paper on the floor. The man picked up his newspaper, stood up, and walked out of the cafeteria.

Being the curious person I was, I went over to his table and picked up the paper from the floor. The note had the name "Professor Jones" on the outside. I opened the note, and it said, "Beware! There comes a time in a man's life when he becomes accountable for the things he has done. You will never know what corner I'll be on and when it will be your turn to answer for the things you have done." There was no signature, only the implied threat of either harm or another kind of retribution. *What would that be?* Just another mystery. I wanted to find out what happened to Al Pedosta and what the other two young men knew about it. But first, I needed to call Dr. Lajonque to see what he'd found out.

I walked back to my car. There sure were a lot of students there for such a small college. Driving back to my house, I noticed the same car behind me that I saw in the parking lot across the street from my house. *Okay, what is going on? Is this person just going over to the hotel, or what is the deal?* I decided that if he continued to sit in the car and stare at my house, I was going to go over there and ask him what he thought he was doing.

As I parked behind my house, I saw a shiny object next to the fence. I got out of my car, walked over to fence, and picked it up. The object was a woman's silver compact. *This must have been in some trash someone was throwing away and it fell from whatever they were carrying.* There was an initial

THE *House* ON THE CORNER

carved on the front, only this wasn't an engraved initial put there by a jeweler; it is carved with a knife. The initial was "B." *Not sure what the "B" stands for.* On the back of the compact was the price sticker. It said, "GC Murphy, 25 cents." Now, this was a very old compact. The GC Murphy store had been gone for over twenty years. *Hey, this might just be an antique. I'll have to show it to Dr. Lajonque.* Not that he was an antique expert, but he did know about them. I stopped to get the mail from the mailbox on my way into the house. There were the usual advertisements, but I find an envelope addressed to "The Occupant of 100 W. Main St." Opening the envelope, I found a note that read, "Stay away from corners, you never know who is hanging there waiting. Remember, people who put their noses where they don't belong may smell something deadly." There was no signature on the note.

I put the note with the folded paper I found at the cafeteria. When I saw Dr. Lajonque, I would show the notes to him. Right now, I needed to get some work accomplished.

I turned on the radio, turn it to the easy listening station, and began working on putting my bed together. Finally, my bedroom was coming together. Clothes were put away, shoes were in the shoe holder in the closet, bed linens were in the hall closet, and the curtains were up in the bedroom.

Looking at the clock, I saw it was time for supper. *Mom was right: if you work hard enough you can make time fly.*

Unknown Caller

It was time to shower, get cleaned up, and figure out where I was going to grab a bite to eat. I didn't need something too heavy, just a sandwich or salad, whichever. I was too tired for a big meal.

I decided to go across the street to the hotel restaurant. No sense in wasting gas as I didn't plan on being up late anyway. As I crossed the street, I see the same car in the lot again. This time there was a woman sitting in it. *Oh well*, I thought, *just let her sit there. If it's anything important, I'm sure I'll hear about it.*

I was seated at a table by the window in the back. *Great: I can watch the door and the car both.* The hostess didn't realize she had helped me.

After ordering, I sat back and relaxed. Not thinking about anyone knowing me, let alone being in the restaurant, I saw Dr. Lajonque pull into the parking lot. As he got out of his truck, he saw the woman in the car. He nodded to her and walked across the street into the hotel. He didn't know I was there. He came into the restaurant, looked around, and walked up to the bar and sat down. He ordered a drink and an appetizer and pulled out his cell phone. It looked as though he was checking his messages. Suddenly, he sent deathly white, pulled out his billfold, laid some bills down, and left.

He was practically running to his truck. I knew it this wasn't just an emergency vet call. What was even more

THE *House* ON THE CORNER

puzzling was as he was leaving, the woman in the car in the parking lot left right behind him. *What is going on?*

The waitress brought me the menu. I ordered my meal and watched the activity in the restaurant. After I ate, I decided to go for a walk. As I walked toward the middle of town, there were three young men on skateboards riding down the sidewalk. All were laughing and having a great time but not paying attention to the people on the sidewalk. Practically running into me, one brushed past me. I thought, *That was just too close for comfort. Isn't there a law about riding skateboards on sidewalks?*

As I continued walking, something felt odd in my pocket. My keys were in my other pocket with my billfold, so I put my hand in my pocket and felt something in it. If felt like a crumpled piece of paper. I pulled it out and flattened it in order to be able to read it. The note said, "Go back to the farm, you'll be safer there. Only bad things will happen to you if you stay in the house on the corner." *Yeah, right, I'm going to flee my house like something out of an Alfred Hitchcock film.* I decided to go home. As I walked behind my house, one of the young people I saw at Ashball College was sitting on the porch of the house across the alley from my house. I decided to introduce myself to my neighbor.

"Hello, my name is—" Just as I started to talk to the young lady sitting there, she stood and went into the house. A very mean-looking young man came to the door and shouted at me. "What in the hell do you want, lady? Whatever you're selling, we don't want any. If you want directions, go to the library or post office or Triple A. We aren't the information bureau around here, and we don't appreciate anyone coming on our property. Do I make myself clear?"

"Oh, yes, very clear. Now, I'm not sure what your problem is, sir, but whatever it is, please be advised I'm your neighbor. I haven't done anything to you to cause you to be so rude to me, nor do I understand what in the world is wrong with this town and the people in it. I have never seen anyone so rude as the young people here. If you have anything you would like to tell me from now on and into the future, you may leave a note in my mailbox. I'm sure I will find it!"

Returning his ugly glare, I turned back to my house. Upon entry, I saw a note had been slipped under the door. It read, "Call me when you get home. Got some news about the bones. By the way, where have you been and what did you find out?" It was signed "Dr. Jerald Lajonque."

I called Dr. Lajonque, and he answered on the first ring. We talked for just a few minutes and agreed to meet after the office closed at the restaurant in the Second Read Bookstore just up the street from my home. The bookstore had been around for a very long time. It was family owned, having been started shortly after the Depression—in 1946 according to the faded sign under the eaves. There was a large basement under the bookstore. I knew this as I used to go there when I was a child, and they held special programs for the children in that basement. *How many times did we play "Zorro" or "Superman" or hold tea parties when we tired of being tomboys and wanted to be real ladies?* (Don't worry, the tea parties didn't happen often.)

I decided to work on cataloging my books on the computer. My most prized possessions were my first edition Carolyn Keene books. They were in excellent shape. A professor friend of mine had left them to me in his will along with a thousand other books when he passed away. These books were insured for more than any other possession I owned. *Guess I'm somewhat like a book hoarder. That's not so bad, could be worse. Could be like those hoarders who can't even find a place to sit down in their own house, let alone sleep in a real bed.*

I finally got everything started and began to work diligently. Before I knew it, it was dark outside. I looked at the clock to see I had only fifteen minutes before I was to meet Dr. Lajonque. I ran into the bathroom, splashed water on my face, changed my shirt and pants, sprayed a little perfume on, and combed my hair. I did have the presence of mind to shut down the computer, put the flash drive in my purse, lock the door, and head to the bookstore.

As I got close to the bookstore, a hawk flew in front of my face and soared straight up toward the sky. *What is a hawk doing out this time of night? I thought this predator only hunted during daylight. Must remember to ask Dr. Lajonque about this.*

Little did I know there would be more events that would take place to change the last few days and days to come.

I saw Dr. Lajonque ordering something then walking to the booth to sit down. I walked over to the booth and sat down. "Hi, Doc, did you order my favorite, or did you leave that for me?" I asked.

"Yes, Adler, it's on its way. I've never forgotten. How could I? I'm the one who started you on that when you first came into the office and found me eating it for lunch," he said laughing.

A waitress brought over our drinks. Black coffee and water for both of us. Shortly after, our meal came. Dr. Lajonque had ordered us the same thing: cold slaw and tomatoes. It made for a very healthy meal We didn't say anything, just started eating. When we both finished eating, we ordered more coffee and a small cup of sorbet to top off the meal.

Dr. Lajonque said, "Listen, Adler, I don't know what you think the bag of bones was, whether it was the Airedale in the picture or what, but those bones were not animal. They were human. I've turned them over to the county coroner and notified the police. They will be visiting you first thing in the morning, but I told them I wanted to be the one to tell you. This more than likely was a great discovery as the bones are surely those of someone's son or daughter. These weren't 'old' bones. I could tell from looking at them the person they belonged to wasn't old age wise. The sad part about this is they've been there for a long time. I'm surprised no one has found them before now."

I couldn't move. I just stared at him. *What did I hear? Human bones? A young person? Is he crazy? Is this a cruel joke?* Now it was my turn to take the deep breath and say, "Dr. Lajonque, are you sure? How long do you think they've been there? Could they have been somewhere else and moved to my basement? Could a homeless person have found the bag somewhere, thought it was something valuable and left them in my basement? I don't understand. This is all quite unsettling because you know as well as I do, this person more than likely didn't die of natural causes. This means whoever killed this person might still be in the area. If they remember where they left those bones, they may want to come back."

"Yes, Adler, you're right. I'm going to be here tomorrow when the police visit. I want to sort of watch the traffic and people to see what kind of reaction takes place with the police car sitting outside your door. If you see anything that doesn't look right, just let me know. I'll be at your house around 9:00 in the morning. Have some coffee on. Do you have anything for a light breakfast for a tired, old vet?" he asked. I nodded. When Dr. Lajonque stood up, I stood up as well. He looked at me and gave me that funny old quirky smile of his and gave me a hug. "See you tomorrow morning, Adler," and out the door he went.

I realized I was not breathing well. It felt as though the walls were closing in on me. I had to get out of the bookstore and get some fresh air. *This isn't right! Darn it, I moved to town to be able to be near places where people are so I could go to the movies, library, mall, or whatever, and now, now I am involved in not one murder, but two!*

Dr. Lajonque left the money for our coffee and such on the table. I took it up to the cashier, paid her, and left the bookstore. If he was to going get change back, the person who fixed our snack just made a tip.

As I walked back, I could see my house on the corner. On the front of the second story was a small balcony that extended over the sidewalk. The balcony and the railing around it looked really good. *Maybe I'll put a chair out there and watch the traffic.* I noticed there seemed to be quite a bit of straw in the corner of the balcony. *When I get in the house, I'll go up to the other bedroom to see if there is a door to the balcony and check it out.*

THE *House* ON THE CORNER

When I got to my door, I noticed there was a note in the mailbox. *Oh God, what is this now?* I pulled the note out. It read,

> I know you have been warned about going back to the country and you have not taken this message seriously enough. If you do not get out of town by midnight tonight, you will leave me no alternative. Beware little girl, I'm not joking. You are in a great deal of danger. Pack your bags now and leave!

I'd had it! I was tired of this cat-and-mouse game; tired of people looking at me funny, sitting across from my house in cars and staring at my house; tired of meeting someone and two days later they are murdered and no one seems to be doing anything about it; tired of finding bones in my basement, thinking they are dog bones only to find out they were someone who was murdered; tired of getting notes telling me to "Beware, you're in danger"—in other words, tired of the whole mess!

So, okay, Adler, what are you going to do about it? I'll tell you what I'm going to do about it. I'm going to find out who and what Al Pedosta was, where he was from, and why someone would want to kill him. Then I'm going to find out who the bones in my basement belonged to. I want to know who killed this person and how their bones ended up in my basement as well as what the person who's been sending me these threatening notes has against me. That's exactly what I'm going to do about it!

I unlocked my door and stepped into my living room. As I turned to lock the door, someone started jiggling the door handle. I leaned against the door, shut it as quickly as I could, and threw my deadbolt locks. The person outside my door kept jiggling the door handle. After what seemed like an eternity, they let go of the handle and started banging on the door.

I didn't move. I just stood, frozen in time, waiting on the person's next move. I didn't know who was out there, only that they seemed determined to get my attention.

As I waited on this person to do something, I saw their shadow move away from my door and turn the corner. As I turned, I saw their shadow against my front window. They were looking in my window. I couldn't see who it was, as I had sheers up. I could only see shadows. If I couldn't see them, then they couldn't see me.

I took off running to the stairwell, up the stairs, and into the other bedroom. *Yes, there is a door to the balcony.* I opened the door, stepped gingerly onto the balcony floor, and stepped right on the pile of straw. My foot slipped, and I fall backward into the bedroom. Straw chaff fell from the balcony to the sidewalk below. Pulling myself together, I stood up and looked out the door.

THE *House* ON THE CORNER

A man was running across the street. I could only see the back of his head. He was wearing some sort of dark running clothes. I could make out the words "Under Armour" on the skull cap he was wearing as well as down the back of the jacket. He ran over to the car that had been sitting there since early morning, got in it, and left in about the same type of hurry as he when he ran across the street. *Damn, I can't see the license plate. Better make a note of what this guy looked like.* Even though I couldn't see his face, I knew enough about his build to give a partial description to the police when they came the next morning.

Back in the bedroom, I saw there was paper lying all over in the corner of the room. As I bent to pick up some of the paper, I noticed there was an old credit card under the paper. It was a very old card, but I could make out the name of the cardholder: Annalee Rosen. The numbers that had been on the back were worn off, and the edges of the card were sort of worn too. It dawned on me that this card had probably been used to get into houses that didn't have deadbolt locks on their doors. It made sense now.

Whoever was spending time in my house must have brought their stolen goods in there and divided the goods up, or maybe they just took them to the pawn shop, sold them, and divided up the money. Now, why did I think there was more than one? Could it be I'd seen too many people together and would naturally think they were all in on it together? Well, enough was enough. It was time to get ready for bed. I had to get up early, and I wanted to make sure all my ducks were in a row when Dr. Lajonque came, and I certainly wanted to be together when the police arrived.

I was ready for bed and had just about drifted off when the phone rang. *Who has my cell phone number? I haven't given it to anyone in town other than Dr. Lajonque.* I picked the phone up and looked to see the name on the Caller ID: "Unknown."

Oh, yeah, this is the night something bad is supposed to happen because I didn't go back to the farm. Well, I'll wait and see.

I feel asleep and was resting well when the sound of squealing tires woke me up. I sat up, swing my legs over the edge of my bed, and put my feet on what I thought were my house slippers. It was dark; I couldn't see what was on the floor. I reached under the pillow and fished out my flashlight. I turned it on, and as I looked down, I saw the headless torso of a dead rat. Stuck to the rat was a note that read, "This could have been you. There are a lot of missing heads in this town; don't make yours next. I'm giving you one more chance to leave, so leave NOW!"

My heart was in my throat. How and when did they get in? My house was locked tight as a drum. What in the hell was happening here? I had enough presence of mind to know

THE House ON THE CORNER

the police wouldn't find anything this time of night; however, I really didn't want to be alone. I called Dr. Lajonque, and he came immediately. We decided to stay downstairs. It would be daylight soon, and maybe we could get a few hours of sleep.

I awoke at 6:00 a.m. Daylight was coming. I looked over at the recliner; Dr. Lajonque was snoring softly. I didn't have the heart to wake him up. Gently tiptoeing past him, I went to the bedroom, changed into a pair of jeans and a clean shirt, and went into the kitchen to put on the coffee and wait for the police to arrive.

Dr. Lajonque slept for about an hour longer and woke himself up choking on his snores. He looked a mess. His hair was rumpled, his usually trimmed moustache looked a little out of sorts, and I could tell his mouth was really dry as he smacked his lips.

"Ready for a cup of coffee, Doc?" I asked as he was still trying to get his bearings.

"Well, Adler, what I need is a bathroom, washcloth, and toothbrush. Got an extra one lying around anywhere?"

I got the items he needed to get straightened up and returned to the kitchen. Finally, two police officers arrived and took our statements. They both looked skeptical. They tried to tell me it was just my imagination; the rat had probably been there for a long time as no one had lived there for several years. They kept saying it was probably some kids playing a trick on me. As they kept coming up with scenarios that could not have happened, I started to get angry.

"Damn, is this all you people have to say?" I asked. "Listen, it's not like I was born yesterday or that I'm not bright enough to see what is going on!"

One of the policemen tried not to look me in the eye. (When a person looks at you like this, it usually means they've got something to hide or they're trying not to have to answer you.) He finally opened his mouth and said, "Look, Miss, are you really sure you're not just making this stuff up so you can get a bestseller?" As the police left, assured me they would be watching my house until this is all resolved, one way or another. *Right,* I thought to myself, *I bet you will.*

Dr. Lajonque didn't say much the whole time the police were there. He looked at me and said, "Adler, settle down. Let's take some time and figure out what's going on. This has been happening since the day you moved in. It's been one thing after another."

As he was talking, I noticed a shadow at the door window. I walked over to the door and saw it is only the mail lady. She was putting an envelope in my mailbox. When she left, I went to the door and retrieved my mail. *Now what?* It was an envelope with "URGENT!" written on the top of the envelope in big, crazy capital letters. My name was the only name on it.

THE *House* ON THE CORNER

Dr. Lajonque walked up behind me and watched me open it. In the envelope were clippings from an old newspaper. The first clipping was a picture of a young man who had died. The headlines read: "Man Found Dead in Larosa Creek." The article further stated:

> On or about the 25th of October, the body of a young man who appears to be in his mid- to late twenties, was found floating in Larosa Creek. The body was found by a young couple who, being out for a Sunday evening ride, decided to park their car near the creek and go for a hike and found the body floating near a pile of debris that had been thrown into the creek by someone. The young man's foot was caught between the door of an abandoned refrigerator and an old dresser drawer.
>
> Sheriff's deputies on the scene stated the young man had been in the creek for a few days. There was bruising on the chest and a stab wound visible at the base of his rib cage. No other visible signs of injury were determined at this time.
>
> The body was removed from the scene by the Compton County Life Squad and taken to the

Unknown Caller

Compton County Coroner's office where an autopsy will be conducted by Corner Ralph Sharp.

Further investigation will be conducted by the Compton County Sheriff's office.

The other clippings were about different murders that took place in surrounding counties. All the deceased were considered unknown by the communities where their bodies were found. There were twelve clippings in the envelope. Mostly the victims were young men or men in their late twenties to mid-thirties.

The whole time I standing looking at the clippings, Dr. Lajonque was looking over my shoulder at them. He didn't say anything, but I could hear him breathing. As I read each clipping, it appeared his breathing becomes more rapid. Turning, I noticed beads of sweat had started to form on his forehead. His cheeks were flushed, and it appeared he could hardly speak. Finally, he said, "Adler, I don't know what in the world is going on, why this person or these people whichever, have singled you out, what this house has to do with anything, where these men are from, but I'm sure of one thing: *you* are in danger, and if you can't see that by now, it's time for you to indeed pack up and move back to the country. I sure as the world don't want anything to happen to you. Since the first

THE House ON THE CORNER

day I met you when you brought your Airedale into my office, I had the feeling you would become a good friend. You aren't just a good friend; you're like a sister to me. If you insist on trying to solve this mystery by yourself, well let me tell you something, that won't happen. I will be with you or somewhere you can reach me, and I'll be here in a flash. Do you understand what I'm saying?"

I nodded my head in the affirmative, went into the kitchen, and poured Dr. Lajonque and myself a cup of coffee. I had to get my thoughts together before I talked. I didn't want to sound like a babbling idiot or like someone who was scared to death, but I wanted to sound like I was convinced these people were out to get someone else, not me, as I had just purchased this house. I didn't know all this other stuff went with it, and this kind of stuff isn't quite what I had in mind.

"Okay, then let's get busy. I'm going to be at the police station first thing. I want to look at some of the mug shots. Maybe I can find some of the people I've been seeing. If I do, then I'll call you. If you don't hear from me, you'll know I'm still looking. How's that sound?" I asked.

Dr. Lajonque just stared. I wasn't sure what was on his mind. "Well, Adler, if you think I'll fall for this crock of bull you're feeding me, then you are wrong! You aren't taking any of this as seriously as you should. Do you really believe the people who are leaving you threatening notes are just playing a game? Can't you see what is going on? They are trying to scare you. They believe you know more than you probably do, or you've seen something you shouldn't have and you're trying to figure it out on your own. They don't know you don't have a clue as to what they are doing, who they are, or even why anything that has happened in the past few days has happened."

It was my turn to stare at him as I spoke. "Okay, I understand what you are saying. You have to understand where I'm coming from. I moved here not expecting to find what I thought were dog bones in my basement only to find out they are human bones. Also, I didn't plan on becoming part of a murder, nor did I plan on receiving the kind of threats I've been getting. At first, I thought it was just kids, but now I know it's not, and for whatever reason these people seem to believe I know more than I do, that I've seen something, and if that is true, I certainly want to know what it was I saw."

Dr. Lajonque then said, "Adler, I'm going to send someone to stay with you at night. I want to hear from you every evening before you go to bed. I don't care what time it is; I want to hear from you. I also want to hear from you in the morning. If you're up to it, I'll meet you at McDonald's, and we'll talk there. How's that sound?"

THE *House* ON THE CORNER

I knew it would not do any good to argue, so I agreed. We then drove to the police station, explained what had happened, and they sat me down with the "mug book." I started looking through it and could not find anyone that looked like the people I had seen. Then it dawned on me: *I'm looking in the wrong place, I need to go to another office.*

Leaving the police station, we talked about meeting the next morning at Mickey D's. I walked on to the library. Once inside, I found the newspaper archives.

I looked up the unsolved murders in a five-county area for the past five years. Eureka! There were more than twenty murders in at least three of the five counties. What really stuck out though was the name of one of the victims. His name was Aaron Pedosta. He had been murdered just one year to the day from Al Pedosta's murder. What did this mean, and what connection was there between the two of them? I made a copy of the article, then looked through the archives for anything else related to Aaron or Al Pedosta.

The librarian came to me and informed me they were getting ready to close. I didn't realize how long I had been there. It had become dark outside. Of course, I didn't drive there, so it was either walk fast back to the house or call Dr. Lajonque. Well, I really wasn't that far from home, only about a mile, and I figured I could walk that in about fifteen minutes, so I took off walking. I had no purse with me, only my keys to my house and the papers I had copied as well as about ten dollars in cash in my pocket.

As I was getting ready to cross the street, a truck pulled up at the corner. I had the light so I started to cross. The driver of the truck started revving the engine. I slowed down and looked directly into the eyes of someone who looked a lot like Al Pedosta. I must have looked surprised as he started to laugh and again revved the engine. "Hey, lady, think you're seeing a ghost?" he asked.

I took off running across the street. I ran most of the way home, and by the time I got to the corner across from my house, I was completely winded. I don't think I broke stride once. Thank God I had been a cross country runner in my younger days as I would not have been able to make it otherwise.

When I arrived at my door, I made sure there weren't any notes, letters, pieces of paper, or anything else that shouldn't be there; thank God, there wasn't anything weird or scary lying around. When I got into my house, I turned to lock the door. Just as I had finished locking the door, I looked through the curtain over to the hotel across the street. There standing on the corner was one of the Pedostas.

As long as he wasn't bothering me, I wasn't going to worry about him. I did plan on going back to the library the next

THE *House* ON THE CORNER

day to do some more investigating about the Pedostas. I had to find out just how many there were.

Looking over at the clock, I saw that it is time to telephone Dr. Lajonque. He answered on the first ring. "Adler, what's going on? Is your cell phone on? Have you found out anything? Are you okay? Do you think you'll be all right by yourself tonight?" asked Dr. Lajonque.

I explained everything that happened since I'd left him earlier that afternoon. When I told him about seeing someone who looked just like Al Pedosta, I heard him sigh. "I was afraid of this," he said. "The Pedosta family is a very old Compton County family. The last of the Pedostas, Ed and Mary Pedosta, were very good Catholics and never believed in birth control. They had seven sons and one daughter. All the children's names started with 'A.' Ed always said they used the first letter of the alphabet because he wanted his children to be first in everything they did in life. Hold on, let me see if I can find the announcement of the last party they gave as all the children's names were listed."

After what seemed to be an hour, Dr. Lajonque got back on the phone. "Took a while, but I've got the names right in front of me," he said breathlessly. "The boys were Allen, Aaron, Aminium, Aeropostle, Atome, Anthony, and Astronomie. The girl's name was Adelaide; they called her Addie. Addie was not just pretty, she was beautiful. She had long blonde hair, skin that looked like bronze, and eyes so blue, you felt as if you were getting lost just looking into them. She was tall, strikingly beautiful, and with all this going on with her, she went to Stewarts Photography, had a portfolio made, and went to New York City to become a model. She was picked up by *Bosofino*, the fashion magazine, and has been their top model for the last few years. She came back for the last party and hasn't been back since. If I remember correctly, the party turned into a disaster. I'll tell you more about it in the morning. Now, are you sure you don't want me to send Nila over to stay with you tonight?"

"Nope," I said. "I can make it tonight. All the doors and windows are locked. My cell phone is charged, and I'm about ready to get ready for bed. As tired as I am, I'm sure I'll be asleep before my head hits the pillow."

We talked a little more, set the time to meet the next morning at McDonald's, and hung up. I got ready for bed and had just pulled the covers up when I got curious and decided to look out the window. My window faced the street, and I could see the corner where the hotel sat. The Pedosta man was gone, but unsurprisingly, the black car was sitting in front of the hotel. I still couldn't tell if anyone was in it, but there didn't appear to be. *Oh, well, I'm going to sleep. I'm tired.*

Suddenly, I was awake. There was sunlight shining in my eyes. *What the hell? I just went to bed.* I threw off my covers, swung my legs and feet around, and stepped on the floor. As I turned around, the alarm clock started to ring. *It's 7:00 already? The night sure went fast. I have to hurry to meet Dr. Lajonque at 7:30.*

Arriving at McDonald's, I saw Dr. Lajonque sitting in a booth. He had two cups of steaming hot coffee in front of him along with what appeared to be breakfast sandwiches. "Well, Adler, while you were slumbering away, I went to the internet. Thought I would save you some legwork. Had to be awake early anyway. Mrs. Brown's old cat thinks she's in heat and was running around the neighborhood trying to find a boyfriend. She never did take being spayed. Her body did, but her mind didn't accept it. Mrs. Brown called, so I went in search of her. Found her behind Minute Deli and Meats sitting on a garbage can singing for the boys. She let me catch her, so she's at the hospital in a cage until Mrs. Brown comes to get her. We go through this about once a quarter. Now Pillesly will be okay for a while." He laughed as he was telling me this.

"Well, Dr. Lajonque, are you going to tell me what else you found, or are you going to make me guess?" I asked.

"All in good time, Adler, all in good time. Let's just eat our breakfast, and we'll talk over coffee."

I don't think I've ever eaten as fast I did then. I was usually a slow eater, enjoying every bite and, if it is especially good, letting the food lie on my tongue as I savor every morsel. I looked at Dr. Lajonque. "Are you finished?" I asked. Dr. Lajonque answered, "Yes, Adler, I'm finished. Get a refill on our coffee and we'll go outside to the table there in front of the restaurant. We can talk there without everyone in the building listening to us."

It was a cold, brisk morning. The sun was beginning to ascend in earnest. This was the kind of day all people who love the fall season would just be giddy about. Good thing I wore a jacket with a hood. If it got too windy, I would pull the hood up over my head.

Dr. Lajonque explained that Ed Pedosta had moved to the Compton County area right after the Vietnam war. He'd worked for a French air company as a pilot flying the boxcar airplanes hauling freight from the USA to France and bringing return freight back to the USA. It was on one of the flights over to France that Ed met Mary Shawleese. She was an art student on holiday in Paris and was in a small gift shop searching for something to bring back to an ailing grandmother in the States. Ed was there to buy something for a girlfriend whose birthday he had forgotten. He wanted to stay in her good graces, so he thought he could make up for the forgetfulness. Sadly, the present was never bought because he took one look at Mary, and, as they say, "That's all she wrote." He was in love, and he knew nothing from that point on would ever be the same.

Mary and Ed started dating and were married some months later. Their first child, Atome, was born in Paris, France. The rest of the children were born in Pedeaux. After working for this company for about twenty years, Mr. Pedosta lost his job with the French air company. He became a pilot for a small company flying freight overseas to remote locations in Europe. He was gone a lot, and after many years of doing this, he decided he wanted to stay in the States to be home with his wife and children.

I listened closely, then asked, "Are the parents still living, and if so, are they living here, or did they move somewhere else? What happened to the rest of the children? I know you told me about Addie, but what happened to the other seven boys?

Dr. Lajonque explained the parents had been killed in an automobile accident a few years after Ed quit flying overseas. By that time the children were pretty well grown. The five older boys and Addie went off on their own. Al and Aaron ended up with a neighbor who was a professor teaching art appreciation at Ashball College. There, Al and Aaron would find their niche. Each boy was born with a natural ability for art. Al's was as a sketch artist. He could take one look at you and draw you in pencil on sketching paper. Aaron was an oil painter. He loved landscapes. He painted pictures Monet would have fallen in love with.

"Why these two young men have been murdered is beyond me, but knowing your penchant for finding out why things happen the way they do, I'm sure you plan on finding out. Now, the other boys have moved here and there. The last I heard, Aminium, they call him Ami (pronounced like amity), joined the Navy. As far as I know he's still there.

"Aeropostle moved to Kansas, and last I heard, he was a manager at one of the Walmarts there.

"Gossip had it Atome moved to France and was living in a village there. He attended college there and became a writer. He hasn't been back that I know of. I don't know what happened to Astronomie and Anthony. Haven't seen or heard from them for a couple of years now."

Dr. Lajonque continued, "I got a call from one of my friends who works at the Moore & Eastbrook funeral home. It appears Al's and Aaron's bodies were moved there at the request of their sister Addie. Don't know why that is, but they're showing them tomorrow night, and the funeral will be on Tuesday morning at 10:00 with the burial of Aaron at 11:00. The funeral home will be taking Al's body to the school as he requested. Got any questions?"

"Of course I have questions! But first, we need to do some more digging. I want to know what these two young men

THE *House* ON THE CORNER

have in common that would cause someone to want to kill them. We also need to find the two guys who were talking with Al the very first day I moved into my house and then later near your office. What's the deal with them? I take it you're planning on going to the visitation and funeral; would it be a problem if I tagged along? This way I can see who else shows up," I stated matter-of-factly.

We talked a little while longer, mainly discussing the possibility of me hiring an assistant to help me with the new book I was planning on writing. The nice part of writing a book in a small town was having a publisher in the town that was interested in your work. It made it all the more special.

Dr. Lajonque agreed to meet me at my house at 6:00 the next evening. From there we would walk the one block to Moore & Eastbrook funeral home, after which we would go back to the hotel for a bite to eat and some more conversation.

I always enjoyed talking with Dr. Lajonque. From the very first day I met him when I took my Airedale to him as a puppy for shots and worming, I found him fascinating. I don't mean this in a sexual sort of way, but more of an intellectual sort of way. He was very charming with his rumpled hair and rough exterior. He diagnosed my dog with congenital kidney disease and told me he wouldn't live very long. Of course, I didn't believe him and took my dog straight to OSU Veterinary Hospital in Columbus, where they diagnosed him the same way. Between the vets at OSU and Dr. Lajonque, my Airedale was able to live for twenty-six months, fourteen months longer than they thought he would.

When my Airedale died, Dr. Lajonque sent me a card expressing his sympathy. I knew how much he liked my dog. During all this time of him treating my dog, we became good friends. After my dog died, I adopted two silky terriers and a shih tzu. Dr. Lajonque has taken care of Sadie, Sophie, and Daisy ever since.

After I left Dr. Lajonque, I walked over to the bookstore. There in the deli sat the two young men who had been with Al. I decided this was a good time to find a magazine, book, or something and get a cup of coffee and a doughnut. I would get a booth not far from them and listen to their conversation (that is, if they were talking loud enough).

I picked up a forensics magazine, got my coffee and doughnut, and sat down in the booth right behind them. *Talk about luck.* They were speaking loud enough I could understand every word. I thought to myself, *Thank you, God, for this.*

I learned the taller of the two was named Simon. He had dark hair and was very thin. The shorter one's name was Michael. They were talking about something that would happen tomorrow.

THE *House* ON THE CORNER

Michael said, "Man, you know we've already proved ourselves to those dopes. Why do we have to do anything else? Man, if Al were still here, we wouldn't be doing this!"

Simon said in a very angry tone, "Shut up, Michael. I'm tired of your whining. Don't you see this is the best thing for us? If we can pull this off, we're in. If not, our best bet is to get out of town as when the others find out what we did and it didn't go right, we're gonna be dead meat. We won't be any better off than Al and Aaron."

After a pause, their voices became a whisper. I could hear paper rattling. I assumed they were preparing for the next day. The last thing I heard Simon say was, "I'm going to head to Lowe's and get what we need. Meet me back at the corner of Main and Oak at 4:00 tomorrow. Go home and get some rest. I need you to be alert and ready to move fast. Understand what I'm saying?"

They stood up and left. I walked over to the window to watch the direction they were going. Michael ran behind the buildings across the street, and Simon walked toward my house. I hurried up and paid my bill and ran out the door, following Simon from a distance to find out where he was going.

It was kind of hard for me to keep up with him as he was tall and had long legs, but again, with my cross country training I wasn't too far behind but far enough he wouldn't see me. He went into a house about three blocks south of my house. *Wait a minute, this is the homeless shelter. What's he doing there?* This guy was a college student; wouldn't he be living in the dorm there?

I waited around a little while. When he didn't come back out, I walked up the street toward my house. I noticed there was a house for sale on the corner. It was a brown sandstone house with a brown serpentine wall. I decide to call the realtor on Monday, as something told me this house had something to do with all this stuff going on.

I didn't see any more of Simon, so I went home and worked on my laundry, house, and other chores to get ready for the next week. I also wanted some time to work on my book.

As I was getting my computer ready to start writing, my phone rang. It was Dr. Lajonque. I answered the phone, and he said in a very excited voice, "Adler, what are you doing? Get yourself together; we're going for a ride. I'll pick you up shortly, so hurry and get ready. I've just passed Ashball College, so I'm almost at your place. Hurry and be on the corner ready to jump in the truck!" With that, he hung up.

I hurried and got dressed, grabbed a jacket and flashlight—don't know why I grabbed a flashlight—and I was on the corner when Dr. Lajonque pulled up.

"Hurry, Adler, hurry" he said as I tried to climb into his truck. Is it my fault my legs weren't as long as his and he

THE House ON THE CORNER

was driving a Ford King Ranch dually without a step on the passenger side? Clearly he wasn't planning on having many people ride with him when he bought this truck.

"What's going on?" I asked as Dr. Lajonque drove out toward the lake. "There's been another murder. A young man's body was found floating in the lake. He is naked. The only thing the sheriff told me was they found what appears to be his jeans lying on the beach. In the pocket was a note with your name and address on it. The sheriff knows you've been asking questions about Al and Aaron, so he wants you out there."

When we arrived, the yellow crime scene tape was stretched across the beach all the way to the picnic tables near the trees. We got out of the truck, and Sheriff Winegard walked toward us. When he got to where we were standing, he explained how the body was found. What was puzzling him was the note he'd found in the pants pocket of the jeans of the young man. It was scribbled in what appeared to be a child's printing. The only thing it said was "Mercedes Adler, 100 W. Main St." The writing was made with a magic marker.

"I don't know why he had my name and address," I said. "I've never seen him before, nor have I written my name and address down for anyone."

Sheriff Winegard looked at me for a long time. I didn't move, and neither did he. Finally, he said, "Ms. Adler, what is it you're looking for? I've gotten word that you are asking lot of questions around town about the Pedostas." All business now, the Sheriff said, "I think you need to leave the investigating up to us; we know what we're doing."

I just looked at him and didn't say anything. I thought to myself, *Let him think what he wants. I know what I'm doing, and I'm going to find out what is going on.* I stood there and let my thoughts take over. I don't know how long we had been standing there before Dr. Lajonque said, "Adler, I think we need to move. The sheriff just called for the coroner. They want to get the body over to the morgue. I want to get you home; you don't look so good."

"It was hard enough to see another person murdered and now you tell me I don't look good?" I looked at Dr. Lajonque and started walking away from the crime scene.

The coroner's vehicle had just pulled up. The door opened, and out stepped Dr. Iles. He was the coroner from Bradey County, the county next door to us. *What happened to our coroner and his assistants?* I wondered as we started toward the truck. Dr. Iles spotted Dr. Lajonque and called, "Hey, Gerry, it's good to see you! Seems like your good coroner has taken some time off, so your sheriff called me and asked me to fill in. Want to help me with this scene? I know it's not an animal, but you never know. You may learn a thing or two," he said with a laugh.

THE *House* ON THE CORNER

"Yeah, I bet I could, but not today. I need to take Adler home. I think this is getting to her. She's not used to this kind of thing. She's seen more since she's moved here than she's seen since she's been alive," Dr. Lajonque stated.

As we were leaving, two more sheriff's cruisers pulled in. One was marked "Investigation Unit," and the other was a regular marked cruiser. Dr. Lajonque looked at them and said, "These investigators have to be careful when they come to what appears to be a crime scene. Just by looking they can't be sure if the deceased is the victim of a homicide or if they died from other causes. Sometimes, the body and scene will indicate murder, but in some cases, all you know for sure is you have a dead body."

My thoughts were racing. "Did you know who this young man was?" I asked.

"No, not really. He looks as though he's from around here. You know, the blonde hair, thin build, like a million other college students that come here," Dr. Lajonque answered.

The rest of the ride was silent with each of us thinking about these young men and what was going on. When I arrived home, I went to my computer. I hadn't set it up after the tech crew had connected me, but it didn't take long to set up a wireless laptop. I was able to connect to the internet and pulled up the local police. It listed the new crimes that had

Unknown Caller

taken place in the past year. I then looked for common factors among the crimes, and it was here I found the following:

1. Two other young men had been killed in the past two years.
2. All appeared to have the same types of injuries and wounds, and all appeared to have been killed by blunt trauma and/or strangulation.

This wasn't much, but I saw seven clear paths forward:

1. Will have to check forensics to see if facts of the cases had been annotated.
2. Find out the latent evidence to ascertain the type of weapon used as well as check sheriffs' records in the counties involved to see if they have shared information with each other as two of the young men were from town and the other was from the country.
3. Talk to some of the students at the college. See if the deceased left an impression.
4. Create a profile of the victims.
5. If necessary, recreate the event for evaluation purposes.
6. Talk with the coroner for autopsy findings.
7. Check the statements with the facts.

THE *House* ON THE CORNER

After putting together this list, I felt better as now I had something to work with. I absolutely hated to fly by the seat of my pants to try to find out why this all was happening and why I would have to become a part of it.

I checked my phone and saw I had enough time to go to the police station. Once there, I would ask for a copy of the investigating officer's report. While I may not have had a legal right to this, I believed I could use my status as an author and try to be honest enough to tell them about the notes and events that had occurred up to and including the most recent homicide. What I didn't know was the police were looking at me for information as much as I wanted information from them.

The police station wasn't that far from my house. In fact, it was in the next block over in the City Building. You had to enter from the back of the building. It was just after 6:00 p.m. when I walked in. It was very quiet, more like a library than a city police station. It was very clean, almost painstakingly clean. There was a tall counter, behind which a lady in a uniform was sitting.

She looked at me with the look of an old school teacher. One eyebrow was cocked, the other in a semi frown. "Can I help you?" she asked.

"Hi, my name is Mercedes Adler. I live at 100 W. Main Street here in Pedeaux. I just moved here from the country. I have received several written and verbal threats. I don't know what is going on or why these are happening to me, but I want to make you aware of them. The first day—" I was stopped by the sudden movement of her hand, like you would use directing children to cross the street.

"No use going through all this now. I'm just manning the desk till the other person gets back from supper. You'll need to speak to Captain Daniel Lawson. He's out as well, and we don't expect him back till tomorrow," she said in a less than compassionate voice.

"Why, may I ask, do I have to wait for Captain Lawson? Isn't there someone else I can file this report with? Are all reports taken by Captain Lawson only?" I inquired.

"No, he's not the only one, but he's the one you will want to talk with." She said. "You understand, don't you Ms. Adler, we've had some homicides here in the past few weeks, and for some reason, your name has been brought up in conversation about those homicides on more than one occasion. The only reason I know this much is I have sat in on a few of the meetings regarding you being seen at the college and you being seen at different places in town, asking questions. In other words, your inquiries have made someone nervous. This is why I want you to talk with Captain Lawson."

"Fine," I said. "I will be back tomorrow morning at 8:00. Will he be here then?"

THE *House* ON THE CORNER

She stated he would and that she would leave him word that I was going to be there. I left there thinking it was too bad a person couldn't even go to a library or a college cafeteria and ask a few questions without it becoming a crime in itself.

When I got back home, the local paper was lying on my stoop. I picked it up. The headline read, "Another Murder in Pedeaux." It went on to say, "Yesterday afternoon at 2:39 p.m., the body of a young man, age 30–35, was found in the woods near the entrance to the former Chess Drive-In movie theatre. No identification was found on the body. Investigation is continuing."

How odd, I thought, that there wasn't more detail than what I just read. Looking at my watch, I saw it was late, and I was suddenly tired. I decided to forego anything else but a hot soak in the tub and then a night of undisturbed sleep. At least, that was the plan.

After the bath and getting into my pajamas, I headed down to the kitchen to get a cup of coffee. As I entered the kitchen, I saw the red and blue lights of a patrol car through the blinds in the window. Walking over to the window, I moved the blinds up. I could see outside where the police had two people up against the patrol car, and they were patting them down.

CHAPTER 10

Unknown Caller

When they'd finished, one of the policemen got on his shoulder mic and called someone. By that time, they had the two people in handcuffs and had put them in the patrol car. The policeman finished talking into his phone and turned to the other one. I don't know what was said, but they both got in the car and drove away. I watched for as long as I could, but I couldn't tell where they were going.

Oh well, I thought, *probably just some kids getting into trouble. Bet I'll find out more about them than they want me to know when I go to the police station the next day.* I closed the blinds and got my coffee. As I headed over to my desk to work on my book, the phone rang. The person on the other end of the phone said, "Beware, beware, beware! There are people who want to hurt you bad, very bad. You won't know where, when, or how, but you must be careful. Stay away from people you don't know. Stay with people you do!" the voice said.

I was so fed up with these threats. Talking with the most authoritative voice I could muster I said, "Thanks for calling, but I don't think this is your problem so I'm hanging up. Don't bother to call me again!"

I was beginning to wonder if this would ever stop. Why in the world was I such a threat to these people, and what in the world did I have or know that would intimidate them to the point of threats of bodily harm?

I walked over to the front window, moved the curtain back, and looked across the street. For the first time since I'd been in the house, there wasn't a black car sitting in the parking lot. In fact, the only car in the lot belonged to the priest who lived in the house next to the church. Maybe tomorrow morning before I met Dr. Lajonque, I'd go over to the church and meet the priest. After all, I'd only been there a short period of time, and who knows? I may like what his church had to offer.

Everything seemed to be settling down. I decided to run a hot tub, fill it full of peach bath spirits, and light a few candles. I turned the cd player on with a little Barbra Streisand playing in the background.

Once in the tub, I began to relax. My muscles had been so tight that at times they seemed to jump when I moved my legs. I must have fallen asleep; a noise downstairs startled me awake, and I noticed the water was ice cold.

I got out of the tub, dried off, and put on my pajamas. During the past week, I'd had the presence of mind to get a few flashlights and put them in strategic spots throughout the house. This way, no matter where I was if the lights went out, I would still have a light in the house.

Picking up the flashlight—not so much for a light but as a weapon if need be—and making sure I had my cell phone in case I needed to call the police, I walked down the steps to the front living room.

Sitting on my couch was Dr. Lajonque. "How did you get in here?" I asked.

"Well, Adler, you gave me a key when you first bought the place. You said I might need it if you were out of town and I needed to take care of your dogs. The reason I stopped is to tell you what I've found out. Didn't want to wait till tomorrow, as I think you will be surprised," he said.

After I sat down, Dr. Lajonque proceeded. "It appears the three boys—Al and Aaron Pedosta and the young man found in the lake—all had something in common. While one might think they were all involved in drugs, this is not the case. All three were involved heavily in the new dance studio called 'Broadway on Broadway,' which is being put together in the old school on Broadway Street. The building was once

THE House ON THE CORNER

owned by Lexia Boardenbach, a well-known dancer from Ukraine. She married the former president of St. Francis school for young men. When Lexia and Burton Boardenbach were killed in a skiing accident in Vale, Colorado, they left the building to Marion Pedosta and Marie Star. These two women were former pupils of Lexia. In Lexia's will, she left a trust to keep the building intact and allow for the upkeep of it. She also wanted it renovated into the dance studio and the performance auditorium she wanted it to be."

"Okay, but I don't see what this has to do with murder," I said.

"Just continue to listen, Adler, then you'll see. Bad luck seems to have followed these two ladies. They started the renovations and decided to take the one possession that was the most sacred piece of art Lexia Boardenbach owned. This art she left to the two Ms, Marie and Marion. Marie and Marion took the art piece to their home, and yes, before you ask, they lived together and had maintained the same address since high school. Even when they went to college, they lived in the same house. You have to understand, as good of friends as they were, they were not lesbians. If anything, they should have been nuns. Neither needed a man, and they let you know it. They didn't seem to be interested in physical pleasure." Dr. Lajonque paused as if in thought, then continued.

"The two Ms decided to take a vacation. They had a bucket of places they wanted to go and things they wanted to do before they died. Well, this time they went to Paris, France. Neither had ever flown before, and on the day they left they were like two little schoolgirls. Both were giddy, talking about where they would visit and joking that maybe one of them would bring back a live Frenchman. They both laughed liked drunken sailors. Had I known that would be the last time I would see them alive, I would have spent more time with them. Marie owned a purebred standard French poodle named Sara. They brought her to me to board until their return. She is wonderful. Black with a white spot at the end of her chin. On the second day of their journey in France, a car came across the center line and hit their taxi head-on. Both ladies were thrown from the car and died on impact with the ground."

"What happened to the other driver? What happened to Sara? Did these ladies have any relatives? Was there a will? When did this happen?" I asked.

"All this took place a few years ago. There was a will, which said their home was to be sold immediately following their burial. All the money garnered from the sale of the house was to go into a trust for the renovation and upkeep of the dance studio. Any furniture, artwork, and other items were to go to the college with the exception of the one piece of art which Ms. Boardenbach had bequeathed to them," he said.

Looking at Dr. Lajonque, I asked, "Where is the house, and what was the one piece of art?"

Dr. Lajonque cleared his throat, stood up, and excused himself while he went to the restroom. When he returned, I could see he had two pictures in his hand. Handing them to me, he said, "You will understand what I've been talking about."

Looking at the first picture, I caught my breath. It was my house! "Are you kidding?!" I exclaimed. "This is my house, you mean they lived here, all this time? If this is true, how did the Airedale get in the basement?"

Before he could answer, I looked at the second picture. It was a pair of tap shoes. They had a lot of "bling" on them, and it appeared the soles were painted gold.

Dr. Lajonque was studying my face, and then he said, "Not sure what to make of the picture? Well, the shoes are tap shoes. The tap on the end of the shoes is made of solid gold. The soles were painted gold. The heel taps were solid gold as well. The 'blings,' as you people call them, are actually one-carat diamonds. The straps are pure silver. In other words, this pair of dancing shoes are worth over one billion dollars!"

"Are you serious?" I said in disbelief. "Where are they now? What happened to them? Were they given to the school as well?"

"That's the problem: they were never found. After the will was read and people found out about the shoes, people kept breaking in and tearing the house up trying to locate them; however, wherever the shoes are, no one could find them," Dr. Lajonque said.

"What about the attorney for the estate? Wouldn't he have had some say in this? Wouldn't he have had some idea where the shoes are? You told me they didn't have children; were there any other relatives?" I inquired.

Dr. Lajonque took a deep breath. "No, no other relatives. They were both only children, and their parents were gone. As far as the attorney, he was killed following a divorce gone bad. He had been the divorce attorney for Angelique Chesner. Her soon-to-be ex-husband hated her attorney as he had found a loophole in the prenup and the probate judge set her up so she would never have to worry about money, a place to live, or a car to drive. What it left Trey Chesner was virtually nothing but a lot of bills that would come due every month. His anger kept raging until one day, Angelique's attorney, Harold Christen, was coming out of his office on the way to the courthouse when Trey walked up to him, pulled out a .38, and shot him square in the back of the head. Harold never knew what hit him. He was dead before he hit the sidewalk.

"Trey then walked into the sheriff's office in the courthouse and told them what he'd done. He was arrested on the

THE *House* ON THE CORNER

spot. In his trial he just smiled at Angelique and said as he walked out of the courtroom, "Well, Angie, looks like you'll have to work. Maybe you can get your old job back trying to find another rich sucker." He was put in prison and was killed during a fight in the dining hall. The kicker was he was killed by Angelique's second cousin, who was a guard there. They never could prove that the killing was intentional. Her cousin moved out of state and hasn't been back. Angelique inherited what was left of Trey's estate as the divorce wasn't final when he died. She moved over to Paris, France, to live with an elderly relative. That's been some time ago, and we haven't seen her around here since. It's my understanding the estate with all his real estate holdings and other interests amounted to around $15 million. I don't know why he thought she wouldn't find out what he had, but she won out in the end."

I had been listening intently, and when he finished talking, I said, "So, you're telling me the shoes were never found. No one knows where they are, and they could very easily still be here. Is that correct?"

Dr. Lajonque nodded his head. Speaking slowly, he said, "Now don't be like all these other treasure hunters and start tearing up your house trying to find them. Many people have already tried and have not been successful. Don't become one of them. It is my guess they are over in Switzerland in a safe-deposit box in a bank and no one will ever find them."

Unknown Caller

There was a knock, and Dr. Lajonque went to the door and opened it. The person on the other side, "Hi, my name is Tommy Smith. I live next door and noticed there's been quite a bit of activity over here. I just wanted to make myself known to the person who bought the house and tell them if they needed any type of help—and I don't have to work—I would be more than happy to make myself available to assist. Are you the person who bought the house?"

Dr. Lajonque moved away from the door and pointed at me. Tommy Smith looked at me and smiled. I smiled back and thanked him for stopping by and assured him if I needed help, I would give him a call. He stood in the doorway for a moment, looked around, and turned and left. Funny thing though, he didn't give me his phone number.

Dr. Lajonque stepped through the door, on to the stoop. He watched Tommy walk down the street. He didn't go to the house next door though; he was walking farther away from it. Then he stopped, turned around, saw Dr. Lajonque watching him, and took off running down the street. Dr. Lajonque watched him until he couldn't see him anymore.

When Dr. Lajonque came in, he said, "I don't want you here by yourself, Adler. There's something going on, and I want to know what it is. Until then, I'm going to stay here at night unless you have a friend or someone else you want to stay with you."

THE *House* ON THE CORNER

"Well, let's put it this way. I could call an old friend to stay, but then I would have to go through all this to bring her up to speed where we are. That would take too much time, and I have a feeling we're getting close to the end, so I want you to stay. I'll make up the other bedroom for you," I said in my most authoritative voice.

Dr. Lajonque nodded. I knew he had to go back to the office, tie up a few loose ends, and gather up his essentials for the next day. When he left, I just collapsed in the chair and sighed the biggest sigh I could muster. A thousand things began running through my mind. *How did all this come to be, and why am I even involved in it?* I got and began cleaning up when there was a knock on the door.

Going over to the door, I looked through the corner of the curtain. As I started to open the door, the door was pushed open against me. There standing in front of me was the biggest, ugliest man I had ever seen. His breath was enough to kill a person, and he wasn't even talking! Finally, he said, "My name is Bryan Kimball. My grandmother owned this house, and I used to come here and stay with her. I was just wondering if you found any old toys or bottles lying around."

"No, I haven't. What was your grandmother's name?" I asked.

He looked at me as though he would prefer to rip my head off than answer my question. Then he said in a very gentle voice, "Her name was Marion Pedosta."

I had to think; this sure as the world wasn't making sense to me. Dr. Lajonque never told me either of the two Ms had gotten married, let alone had children. I was trying to absorb all of this and getting ready to ask what that had to do with my house or me. Bryan Kimball turned to leave when one of the police cars pulled up at the light.

Bryan saw the car and turned deathly white. He asked if I had a phone or a backdoor. I asked why, and he stated he hadn't done anything wrong. He was just in the wrong place at the wrong time. He kept looking at the police car.

I don't know why, but I felt sorry for this guy. I didn't know him from Adam. He could have been a serial killer for all I knew, but my gut instinct told me he was just a scared young man who needed some help, so I let him in my house and closed the door. The police car went on by, although somewhat more slowly than would be considered normal.

Looking at this young man I said, "Okay, Bryan, let's get down to basics here. First, tell me about your mother."

Bryan asked if he could sit down. When I nodded yes, he sat down and started picking at the threads on the arm of the chair. He took a deep breath and said, "I just found out who my birth mother was last year. It was kinda ironic as I had no intention of coming to this town to go to college. My dream was to go to State College on a wrestling scholarship, but there are a lot of guys out there who seem to wrestle better than me. Even though I wasn't recruited for State, I was recruited for Ashball College. They've given me a full ride as my academics in high school were good, so it looked great to this college to recruit not only someone good in wrestling who filled the weight class they needed but who had a brain as well. Once I got here, I was walking down the street, and this man came up to me and asked me if I knew Marion Pedosta. I told him I didn't, but he said I sure looked like her, and he wondered if I was her son. I didn't tell him I was adopted as I really didn't care at that time who she was. I was raised by a couple from Iowa and was the only child they had. As far as I'm concerned, they are my parents, so who I was 'birthed' by didn't bother me."

"You weren't even the least bit curious as to why a total stranger would walk up to you and ask you these questions?" I asked.

"No, not at all. I'm fresh from farm country. I was taught not to question people you don't know as sometimes they are just running their mouth to try to get information and could say anything," he explained.

Unknown Caller

"Okay, Bryan, you're naïve, you don't ask him any questions at that time, but there had to come a time when you did ask questions. When did this happen?" I said rather shortly.

Bryan stated, "It was the beginning of my sophomore year. We were at a wrestling meet at Heidelberg College. We got there a day early so we could practice to get used to their mats and such. Well, I had a paper due on Monday, so I asked if the library stayed open late. After practice, I went to their library. My paper was on the brick in old buildings. What kind of clay it was, how they made the brick, and the difference between today's brick and brick from the 1950s or before. I had chosen the old building in Pedosta that was being made into a dance studio and auditorium, 'Broadway on Broadway.' I found an old newspaper that showed a really good picture of the brick. I decided to read the story about this building when I found a picture of the owners, Marion Pedosta and Marie Star. Looking at the picture of Marion Pedosta was like looking at myself in a mirror. She was a rather tall woman, with broad shoulders and what looked to be blonde hair. This is when I decided maybe I should start to investigate my birth."

"So, what did you do then? Go to the hospital where you were born, call your adoptive mother and father, turn their world upside down 'cause you're trying to find out about this woman who you first told me was your grandmother, and now you're telling me she's your mother?" I asked.

Bryan's face turned beet red. He stood up, looked at me, and said through clenched teeth, "Listen, lady, by rights, this house should be mine. I know for a fact Marion Pedosta was my mother! If I had told you that, you wouldn't have believed me. I guess we don't have anything else to talk about. I know there's something here that belongs to me, and I will find it." With this, he stomped over to the door, opened it, and left.

I must have sat there for a long time because it was pitch dark outside when I stood up. A million thoughts were running through my mind. I needed to call Dr. Lajonque. I dialed his number. It went to voicemail. *Great*, I thought. Suddenly, he was yelling over his answering machine, "Don't hang up, Adler. Wait till I get this confounded thing turned off. God, I hate these contraptions, don't know why I ever let those girls talk me into this. Now wait a minute … there we go. Okay, Adler, what's up?" he said, breathing heavily.

"First, Doc, you need to cut down on the cigarettes; sounds like you were running a marathon. But this isn't why I called," I said. I then proceeded to tell him about Bryan Kimball and his claim to be Marion Pedosta's long lost son who was put up for adoption and how he says I have something in the house that belongs to him.

Dr. Lajonque then said, "Adler, whatever you do, don't let him in again. You don't know him. You don't even know who he really is. You have to be very careful. It's been in the papers about the Pedosta boys and about the young man they just found. Anyone who even remotely knows about the tap shoes will begin to think they're there, so do me a favor and don't open your door to any more strangers, is this clear? And make sure your doors are locked. I've got an 8:00 emergency coming in or else I would be there, but I'll be there as soon as I'm finished. Go ahead and go to bed if I'm not there by 10:00 and I'll let myself in. We'll talk more in the morning. Just make sure you've locked your doors. I really don't have a good feeling about this Bryan Kimball."

I did as Dr. Lajonque instructed. I locked all the doors and even checked the windows to be sure they were locked as well. I put on the coffee pot as I'd made up my mind to wait up for Dr. Lajonque. I turned on the television and went upstairs to put on my pajamas. Just as I had gotten them on, my cell phone rang. If I don't recognize a number, I typically won't answer, and being I didn't recognize the number, I let the call go to voicemail.

I went downstairs to the library and sat down at the desk. While waiting on the computer to warm up, I remembered I had the coffee pot on and decided to go to the kitchen and get a cup of coffee. As I was getting the coffee cup, I heard a

THE *House* ON THE CORNER

noise in the front of the house. I turned off the kitchen light and walked back into the living room. With the only one light on set at a dim level, I could make out a shadow at the front door. *Oh God*, I thought, *here we go again!* I stood in the living room watching the shadow. It just stood there. I couldn't make out whether it was a man or woman. I could tell one thing for sure: they weren't very tall, only about five foot six or so. This person tried the doorknob, hit the door facing, and left. When I felt they were gone, I walked over to the door, unlocked all the locks, and gingerly pulled the door open. About this time, Dr. Lajonque walked up to the door.

"My God, Adler, what in the world are you doing, trying to get yourself killed?" he demanded.

"Of course not," I replied. "I just saw someone at my door. I was trying to see who it was. Did they leave anything lying around the door? The person stayed here for a long time. I wasn't sure what they were up to."

"As a matter of fact, there is an envelope on the step. It is addressed to you, no return address or stamp," Dr. Lajonque said as he bent over and picked up the envelope. He then handed it to me.

I took the envelope from Dr. Lajonque and stepped back from the door as Dr. Lajonque came in. "What is it, Adler?" he asked.

Unknown Caller

I read the letter inside. It was instructions to go to a town named Eweleste, Ohio, which was just about twenty miles northeast of Pedeaux. Upon arrival there I was to go to Vallcester Farm on Post Road. There was a long driveway that wrapped around the home, and I was instructed to park in the back. I was to come by myself. Dr. Lajonque was not invited, nor was I to bring any law enforcement officers. The letter further stated "everything you need to know about the Pedostas and other events" would be explained upon arrival. Should I not follow the instructions, then the writer of the letter could not guarantee nothing would happen to Dr. Lajonque or the citizens of Pedeaux as well as my own three dogs. The writer gave me twenty-four hours to make up my mind. I was expected at Vallcester Farm no later than 6:00 p.m. the next day.

I finished the letter, folded it, and placed it in the envelope. I looked at Dr. Lajonque and said, "It's nothing, only a letter from a young man who saw me at the hotel when I first arrived. He was just expressing interest in going out with me. Of course, I have no intention of acting on his request. With everything else going on, I wouldn't risk the chance this person is really a pervert who just wants to hurt me."

Dr. Lajonque looked at me with the skepticism of a priest who didn't believe the confession of the person in the confessional. The only difference was Dr. Lajonque could see

THE *House* ON THE CORNER

my face; the priest had to rely on the inflection a person's voice to know when they are lying. "Adler, if this is anything that is dangerous or puts you in harm's way, I will be furious with you! Is this understood? I don't know what you are up to, but I won't push you on this. If it has anything to do with the murders of those young men or the tap shoes, I strongly advise you to contact the police. This is really the wrong way to handle things, Adler. You are not a detective. Do you have to go somewhere?" he asked.

"No, Dr. Lajonque, I'm not going anywhere. I'm staying here the rest of the night and getting up early in the morning and working on my house. I've got to get things done in order to get the girls here. If the day goes as planned, I may run out to the farm for a while to check on the house. I need to get away from this for a while. In fact, the more I think about it, the more I think I'll just stay at the farm tomorrow night, so you won't even have to come over," I said firmly.

Again, Dr. Lajonque looked skeptical. "Okay, Adler. Whatever you say. It's getting late. Time to get some rest. See you tomorrow." With that, Dr. Lajonque walked into the bathroom to change for bed.

I headed up the stairs to bed. Once I was in bed and with the glow of the light on the nightstand, I pulled out the letter again and reread it, making mental notes about what I should take with me.

Unknown Caller

The rest of the evening proved uneventful. The next morning, I got up, brushed my teeth, showered, blow dried my hair, and put on my jeans, boots, and a t-shirt. I pulled out a hoody sweatshirt and a jacket, picked up my flashlight and put it in my purse, and walked downstairs to where Dr. Lajonque had left the coffee pot on with a note attached to the countertop. It said, "Got an emergency call. Had to leave. You have my cell phone number if you need me. Talk to you later. By the way, leave me a voicemail if you are definitely not coming back to town tonight." It was signed, "G. Lajonque."

Whew, I thought. *Now I can go on to Vallcester Farm without explanations or having to lie to Dr. Lajonque.*

CHAPTER 11

More Investigation

She walked out of her house, locked her door, and went over to the hotel for some breakfast before her journey. She wasn't sure how long it would be before she'd have a chance to eat again, and she wanted to be sure to get some "stick to the ribs" food. Mercedes went into the restaurant. She looked around and chose the last booth next to the French doors that opened to the patio and sat facing the entrance doors. She'd had an uncle who worked for the FBI. He taught her never to have your back to a window or a door when you're seated in a restaurant so you're always able to see anyone coming toward you. This way there wouldn't be surprises.

After she ordered her breakfast, Mercedes pulled out her notepad. She started writing notes to ask this mystery person she would be meeting later that morning. A man walked in

More Investigation

through the French doors and walked up to the bar, where he sat down. He pulled the menu from the holder, and after ordering, he looked into the mirror that stretched from the floor to ceiling and extended the length of the wall.

In the mirror he saw Mercedes and turned completely around on his stool and stared at her.

Mercedes felt as if someone was watching her and looked up. She saw the man looking at her, and as soon as she did, he turned back around and put his head down as if not wanting to be seen. *God, that's creepy,* she thought. *Hope they hurry up with my food so I can get out of here.*

When her food came, Mercedes ate with abandon, acting as if she hadn't eaten in a year. She was one of those people who could eat ten times a day and never gain weight. After eating, she paid her check and left. The man at the bar paid his check as well and left the way he had come in, through the French doors by the patio.

Mercedes got in her car and pulled out of the parking space in front of her house. She drove southeast for twenty miles as the directions had stated and came into the town of Eweleste. It was a small village with only four stop signs. She was to turn left at the last stop sign onto Chipman Road. She was to follow Chipman to the first road to the right, which would be Vallcester Road, which was a dead-end road that would lead back to Vallcester Farm. She'd been told to go to the back of the farmhouse upon her arrival, where she was to ring the doorbell with three rings, pause, then ring three rings again.

It wasn't hard to find Chipman Road, nor was it hard to find Vallcester Road. All was going well, and this was good, as Mercedes was beginning to get a little nervous about what she was about to do. The drive to the farm was beautiful. A grove of hard maple trees lined the driveway off Vallcester Road. White board fencing behind these trees lined field after field as far as the eyes could see. There were two big horse barns, a tack house, and a large hip roof barn that would hold hay for the horses. But Mercedes wondered where the horses were. *They must be on the back side of the farm or something,* she thought. Funny thing was there was no sign of a horse trailer, truck, or a vehicle of any kind.

When Mercedes parked her car behind the house, she got out, locked her doors, and walked up to the door. She did as she'd been instructed, and after she rang the bell, the door automatically unlocked. Apprehensively, she opened the door and stepped into what looked to be a mud room. There in the corner were gum boots, various riding boots, and other types of equipment. An old jacket with rips in the shoulder was pushed into the corner. She noticed an intercom panel next to the light switch.

Mercedes knocked on the door that she thought would open into a kitchen. A robust woman who looked to be about sixty years old opened the door and informed her with a French accent, "The missus is expecting you. Please follow me."

Mercedes followed this woman through the very old home. The kitchen was retro. It probably had one of the first double ovens ever made. All appliances were turquoise in color. Even with their age, they looked as good as new. Mercedes was taken through the dining room, which had a crystal chandelier over a very beautiful walnut dining table with an arrangement of cut flowers in the middle. The wallpaper was old, but it was in good shape. *Looks like the housekeeper did her job well,* Mercedes thought as she followed her guide. In the living room was a horsehair sofa with a footstool that matched. This sofa looked as though no one had sat on it for a very long time.

Following the housekeeper down a very long hall, Mercedes was impressed with the artwork lining the hallway. There were oil paintings of fox hunting scenes. Most had ornate frames around them, but there were a few smaller ones with walnut frames placed in strategic spots along the wall.

There were a few stands with different types of fox statues and huntsmen. Above the door facing was a pair of riding whips crossed into an "X." Finally, after what seemed a mile-long walk, the housekeeper led Mercedes into a very

THE *House* ON THE CORNER

large library where, in the corner behind a very large desk, sat a very small older woman who was busy working on a computer. The housekeeper cleared her throat, and the lady looked up and said, "Oh, I see you've met Helene. She is my housekeeper, been with me since I was a young girl. You would never know she's seventy-five, would you? You must be Mercedes Adler. I've heard a lot about you from some friends of mine who keep me informed as to what is going on in Pedeaux. You are really stirring up a lot of trouble, and we need to talk."

Mercedes looked at her. "Are you kidding?" she said. "You certainly don't expect me to sit down with you like we are old friends when I don't even know who you are." She caught her breath and she continued, "I may have made a mistake coming here. My curiosity got the best of me as I wanted to see what you wanted. I think I'll head back to Pedeaux. I have plenty of work waiting for me, and I need to get it done." As Mercedes turned to leave, the lady said, "No, young lady, you are not going anywhere until we've talked. You might think this is just a game, but it's not. There are people involved who need to know exactly why you are nosing around. What is it exactly you expect to find?"

Mercedes looked at her and said, "First, tell me who you are and where you fit in this puzzle."

The lady looked at Mercedes and said, "Sit down, Ms. Adler. Helene, please bring me a cup of coffee." Turing back to Mercedes, she asked, "Is there something you want?" Mercedes shook her head no. Nodding to Helene, the elderly lady continued, "My name is Harper Patricia Pedosta. My friends call me H. P.," she laughed. I have lived in this area my whole life with the exception of a few years when I went away to college in France. The college I went to was called *Collége du Moulin Blanc* located in Saint-Tropez. Saint-Tropez was once a small fishing village, but it became a home for artists after the First World War. I learned to paint still life and fell in love with the fox-hunting world, which was where I would find my niche. Being around artists, listening to them, watching them, and of course fox hunting with them was transformative. When I completed my education, I decided to come back home and teach at the college, which I did until my retirement this past June."

"Okay," Mercedes said. "This is all well and good, but what does this have to do with me?"

"In time, Ms. Adler, in time. When you met Al Pedosta, it wasn't just by chance. You'd bought the one thing he always wanted, the house on the corner. That was where Al's relatives lived and where the other woman who lived with them kept many, many secrets. Al had heard about the secrets, and he came out here to visit me to find out what I knew. When

THE *House* ON THE CORNER

he figured out I didn't know anything about anything in the house, he became irritated and wanted to slam something. I ordered him out and told him if he were to ever return, I would call the sheriff and have him arrested for trespassing. Distant relative or not!" She continued, "I didn't tell Al anything he didn't already know. He said he wanted to know about the secrets—what they were. I think he only knew the rumors. I told him if he knew there were secrets, there wouldn't be any secrets because if a person tells you something in private and asks you to keep it secret and you tell someone else, it doesn't remain a secret any longer."

Mercedes waited on her to continue. Ms. Pedosta said, "I do know about a few of the things that the two women didn't want the whole world to know. One of them was the tap shoes that are worth a fortune. They haven't been seen for a very long time. As far as I knew they were in the house right before they went to France. My father saw them and told the 'girls,' as he called them, to get them in a safety deposit box because when people found out about them, they would try to tear the place up looking for them. The other thing the girls showed my father was a complete set of rare first edition Mark Twain books. These books were autographed by Mark Twain, which made them priceless. For a book collector, this would be a wonderful find, not counting just how much they are worth."

"So, you're saying the two most important things that are worth a fortune may still be in my house?" I asked. "What's in this for you? You didn't have to say anything, just let me be and see what happened. Are you expecting to gain from this if I were to find these things?"

Harper Pedosta looked me straight in the eye and a with the conviction of a "hellfire and damnation" preacher said, "If you think for one minute I brought you out here to see if you found these treasures, you are crazier than the rest of those people trying to find them. Don't you understand, Mercedes, I'm trying to warn you to be careful? It is not often I invite someone to my farm. I don't go very many places these days as I enjoy staying right here. If I could have groceries and medicine delivered, I would never leave. Of course, I do keep in touch with the real world through Dr. Gerald Lajonque. He informed me when the house sold and who it sold to. I haven't seen him since the day he came and told me about the sale of the house. I loved it when he told me it sold to a writer, and that the writer was a woman who'd lived on a farm made it even more wonderful. What he didn't tell me was how strong-willed you are. Now, where were we? My hope is you will go back to your home and give up the notion that you are going to continue your amateur detective work and begin making the house on the corner your own. I doubt you have spent a quiet night there since you've moved in, and I'm sure you haven't even unpacked your boxes the movers brought in, have you?"

Mercedes didn't answer her. She just looked at old Ms. Pedosta again and finally said, "If this is all you called me out here for, then you could have said this over the phone. No, I don't believe you. I think you called me out here for another reason, whether it be to find the tap shoes or, for that matter, the books. Either way, you called me here for a reason and I intend to find out what it is."

CHAPTER 12

The Meeting

"The dog picture you found in the basement belonged to Lexia Boardenbach. She loved Airedales. She wanted to breed them, but her family didn't want puppies all around, so she settled for owning one and having him neutered. She named him 'Bogart,' as she was a fan of Humphrey Bogart. Bogart was a good dog, very affectionate and protective of Lexia. One day, she came home from work to find him dead in the basement. Someone had stabbed him and hung him to bleed out, like they do deer, only they hung Bogart in the basement with a note on him. The note told the Boardenbachs to leave town and take the dancers with them."

Mercedes sat there for a long time looking at her before asking, "So, in essence, you're saying the only reason all this happened was someone thought I would find the treasure, this being the dancing shoes and the books? Even if it is true, the shoes and books are worth a fortune; what makes you believe these things were left in the house?"

Ms. Pedosta was nodding as Mercedes was talking. She said, "I know they are there. Before the girls left, they sent me a message telling me to look after the place, they wanted me to be sure no one would try to change the structure of the house in any way. If someone wanted to put paint on the walls, it was okay, but any other structural work would not be approved without their seeing what wanted to be done, so this is what leads me to believe they left these things there, hidden in some remote spot where no one would be the wiser."

The telephone rang. Ms. Pedosta answered, then looked at Mercedes. "Yes, Gerald, she is still here. You want her to wait here for you? I will make sure she does. You'll be here in about twenty minutes? Thank you, Gerald, we'll see you shortly."

Putting her phone down, Ms. Pedosta turned back to Mercedes and said, "I'm sure you heard the conversation, and I assume you know it was Dr. Lajonque? He would like for you to stay here until he arrives. He asked if it would be all right to leave your automobile here. He knows that will be fine with me. It appears he is planning to take you somewhere. I have the feeling it has to do with what we have been discussing this afternoon." As she said this, the corners of her mouth turned up just ever so slightly.

The Meeting

While waiting for Dr. Lajonque, Ms. Pedosta took Mercedes on a tour of her rambling country home. In almost every room there were fox hunting pictures, fox statues, or something to do with fox hunting. In the library there was shelf after shelf of books from England that had fox hunting titles, and many were first editions. Inhaling the aromas of the library, Mercedes thought, *I could stay in this room for the rest of my life*. You could smell the musty odor from some of the books, telling you they were very, very old. She asked Ms. Pedosta, "How long did you fox hunt? Did you ever get to go to England and fox hunt over there? I know here in the US we fox hunt for the sport, not for the kill. We don't see the fox as something that needs to be eliminated."

"You don't have to sell me on the sport of fox hunting, Mercedes. You see, I have spent most of my life on the back of a horse, either showing at horse shows or fox hunting. As you can see, my first love is the fox hunt. Waking up in the early morning hours, getting my flask ready with just a touch of bourbon in some hot tea to basically kickstart the old ticker, dressing in my best hunting attire, and calling my stable hand to ensure the horse was loaded on the trailer, we would set off for the farm where we would meet up with the rest of the group," she said with a faraway look in her eye. She continued, " I stopped riding when . . ." She stopped talking as there was someone knocking on the door. Excusing herself, Ms. Pedosta stepped out of the room.

Mercedes heard Ms. Pedosta thank someone, and she came back into the room with a small package wrapped in tan shipping paper. She handed the package to Mercedes and said, "Mercedes, I don't know what's going on, nor do I want to be a part of it. This package is addressed to Mercedes Adler with my address on the package."

Mercedes looked at her in shock, thinking to herself, *How did anyone know I was here? What is going on?* Opening the package, she gasped. In the box was a picture of an Airedale dog. The dog was standing beside a gentleman who looked very much like Dr. Lajonque. The picture was dated 1945. *What does this mean?* she wondered.

Looking at Ms. Pedosta, Mercedes said, "I assure you, I don't know who knew I would be here other than Dr. Lajonque, but I promise you one thing: I'm just trying to find out why someone wants to frighten me enough to leave my home. I know you've told me about the dancing shoes and the books, but I can't really believe this is the reason that two young people have been killed in the past few days. I think there is more to this than that. You told me you are a distant relative of Al and Aaron Pedosta. That's great, and now you know I haven't found the treasures you describe, nor do I have any intention of looking for them as I don't believe

The Meeting

this is what people are really looking for, nor do I think they are even in my house." Just as I finished this statement, Dr. Lajonque walked into the room. "Hi, H. P." he said. "Well, Mercedes, you ready to go?"

As Mercedes picked up her purse and started to walk toward Dr. Lajonque, Ms. Pedosta said, "Listen, Mercedes, I know you don't believe anything I've told you, but the things I told you are true. You just moved into the house, and in just a few days you have heard things and seen things most people don't see in a lifetime. I'm telling you the truth; the shoes and books may be there, so just be careful. I don't want you to become a statistic as well. Talk to whoever you have to, do what you think you have to . . . but be careful. I hope you are successful in your endeavors, and if you find out who killed my relatives, please let me know. I would be eternally grateful."

When they got outside, Dr. Lajonque said, "I had one of the office girls bring me out. This way I can drive you back to town. I know you'll want to go to the police station and see how the murder investigation is going."

"No, Dr. Lajonque, I don't think so. I think we'll head over to Dr. Sharp's office and get the coroner's report. If you want to go with me, great. If not, then take me to your office, and I'll just go by myself."

Dr. Lajonque looked at Mercedes and said, "If you believe for one minute I'm leaving you alone with all the threats you've received, you're crazy. Let's go see Ralph and see what he has."

The coroner's office was located in a building near the sheriff's office and around the corner from the police station. When we walked in the reception area was empty. No receptionist, just a folded note stating they would return in one hour. I looked at Dr. Lajonque. He was frowning as he headed for a door marked "Employees Only, Do Not Enter." I was right behind him as he pushed the door open and walked down a long hallway. There was a red light on over the door. Dr. Lajonque said, "Someone's in there, this is where they print the photos of the crime scenes or autopsies. We'll wait in Ralph's office till he comes out."

I had just finished reading an article in the *American Journal of Forensics* when Dr. Ralph Sharp walked into his office. Looking surprised to see us there, he grinned and said, "Well, well, what is my favorite veterinarian doing in my office, and who is this you have with you? Now, don't tell me, Gerald, are you planning on getting married and you want me to be your best man?" He then let out a loud belly laugh.

"No, Ralph, not getting married. This is Mercedes Adler. She just moved into the house on the corner of Mulberry and Main, across from the hotel. To make a long story short, she's been a victim of some bizarre happenings that involve her house. We're not real sure if her buying the house has anything to do with the murders of the Pedosta brothers, but it seems to me, there are far too many coincidences," Dr. Lajonque stated very matter-of-factly.

"Well then, what is it you need to know?" Dr. Sharp asked me.

"First of all, what was the cause of death for these two? Then, who came to identify their bodies? Was there anything in common about their deaths other than the fact they were murdered?" I was talking so fast I sounded like an auctioneer.

"Al died of blunt force trauma to the back of his head. Death was instantaneous. He certainly didn't know what was coming. Now, Aaron, he's a different story. There was a small, very minute hole in the back of his ear. Someone had come up behind Aaron and with a very swift and carefully placed syringe, shot enough lidocaine into his system that he was paralyzed instantly. Circulatory collapse followed. His blood pressure fell, and he went into cardiac arrest. Whoever killed these two young men certainly wanted them dead. The one thing I did find they both had in common is the small tattoo each one had at the bottom of their left shoulder blades. It was in the shape of a butterfly, very colorful, but when you actually looked at it, it was designed with a series of numbers, all made very, very tiny in such a fashion it would look like ink lines. I've never seen anything this intricate. It would have taken hours and hours to connect this. The person who

THE *House* ON THE CORNER

did this had to have hands as steady as a rock. There couldn't have been any type of mistakes as it would have looked very amateurish."

Mercedes listened intently as Dr. Sharp explained his findings. The whole time he talked, his facial features revealed a very concerned person who was deeply devoted to these two young men. When he finished, she said, "Dr. Sharp, you seemed to have known these boys quite well. Are you related in some fashion?"

"No, Miss Adler, I'm not related to them. I was a fan of their relative, Lexia Boardenbach. I loved her artistic work and stayed in touch when they left on various trips. When word got back to me the federal government was investigating them, I had no choice but to sever any ties I had with them as I didn't want anything to happen to my reputation or stance here in the community," Dr. Sharp answered.

"I find it hard to believe, Dr. Sharp, you would just stop corresponding with Lexia when you appeared to have been so infatuated with her work. Did the feds come to Pedeaux to ask questions or even come to you for information?" I asked.

Dr. Sharp stood up and, looking at Dr. Lajonque and Mercedes, he said, "I believe I've answered your questions. Now, if you will excuse me, I have work to attend to. Gerald, if you need anything else from me, please feel free to call me.

The Meeting

Anything Ms. Adler may want, she can go through you to find out."

Mercedes walked between Dr. Sharp and Dr. Lajonque and, looking at Dr. Sharp, said in her sweetest voice, "Don't worry, Dr. Sharp, I will certainly go through Dr. Lajonque as you wish. However, I may be also contacting the federal marshals to find out what they were doing here and what was so important they would spend any time at all investigating the Pedostas or Lexia Boardenbach. Also, before I leave, did you happen to take photos of the tattoos on the boys' shoulders, and if you did, may I have a copy of them?"

Dr. Sharp informed Dr. Lajonque he could pick up the photos the next day. Outside, Mercedes asked Dr. Lajonque to take her home. It had been quite a day, and she needed to absorb this all to try to make sense of it. She could have easily walked home but decided she was extremely tired and welcomed the idea of a ride home.

~

I thanked Dr. Lajonque for the ride and the day's events and assured him he did not need to stay with me as I felt as though nothing would happen, and if something did, he would be the very first person I would call. I then closed the

THE *House* ON THE CORNER

door, locked it, and headed to the kitchen, carrying with me the package delivered to H. P. Pedosta's home addressed to me.

Looking into the box, I took out the picture. It was dated 1945; on the back was some writing that was very faint. I retrieved my magnifying glass and set the picture under the lamp on top of my little desk. The light showed the letters N, I, R, and I. It dawned on me that because Pedeaux was a college town, the library at the college was open twenty-four hours a day. Throwing some water on my face, I grabbed my purse and car keys, locked the house, and headed for the library.

Arriving at the library, I found a very pretty young lady sitting at the desk. She was very good at giving me the directions to the history section. I loved this library. At the middle of each section was a laptop computer for the use of students if they were trying to find a specific book. Sitting down at the computer, I typed in the words, "Stolen papers from World War II." Much to my surprise, an article from an Italian newspaper appeared. It was written in Italian. Being that I could not speak the language, I pushed the print button and waited till the computer showed it had finished sending the article to the printer. Going back to the librarian, she handed me the paper I had just printed. She knew by the look of surprise on my face that I didn't know how she knew this was my paper. She explained that all papers sent to be printed by students would come to the printer behind her desk. This way they always knew what the students were printing as well as what they were looking at on the computer, which would also let the library know how much to charge the students for printing. It also seemed to stop students from stealing papers they'd printed as well as cut down on the students looking at websites that were not appropriate.

After paying the modest cost for printing the article, I walked out of the library wondering how in the world I would translate the article. It dawned on me the bookstore at the school should sell dictionaries, but I checked my watch and saw the bookstore was closed.

On the way home, I remembered I hadn't eaten anything the whole day. I was just about ready to order a pizza when the phone rang. It was Dr. Lajonque wanting to know if I was doing okay. I told him I was fine, and he stated he was picking up some food for us and wouldn't take no for an answer. *Great,* I thought to myself, *looks like I won't be able to find out what the article said tonight.*

When Dr. Lajonque arrived, something told me not to tell him about the article. We talked about the visit with Ms. Pedosta, how my dogs were doing at the kennel, and basically small talk. Usually after eating, I would make a pot of coffee and fix some cookies or something for dessert. Tonight, I didn't bother, and pretending I was tired from the events of the day, I scooted Dr. Lajonque out the door so I could do some investigative work on my computer.

I remembered a few years ago I had purchased a program that would translate various languages into English, I put the Italian disk in my computer then scanned the papers from the library into the computer. In what seemed to be magic, the Italian words changed to English. The articles were dated March 23, 1945, and the first one read, "A church in Rome, Italy, reported documents stolen from a Sentinel's office. The documents were reported as being part of an ongoing investigation in the relationship between the secretaries of Mussolini and Hitler. Authorities also report witnesses seeing a tall, broad-shouldered American hurrying from the area just before the break-in was discovered. More details will be released as they become available."

Another article read, "The constable of the village of Venicia reports the documents reported as being stolen were fake. There was no apparent relationship between the secretaries of Mussolini or Hitler. This appeared to be a fabrication perpetuated by two young college students, Alexia Boardenbach and Francine Audincourt. These two young ladies were studying at the College of Venicia. They concocted this after finding the college was about to lose their funding from America. The US Department of Education had decided not to fund American students after the last quarter in 1945. With the loss of the American funds, the college would have closed. The young ladies thought this hoax would keep the college open as it would bring in historians, teachers, and other people of interest who would want to research the relationship of these two secretaries as well as look for other items of interest between Mussolini and Hitler. As no one was hurt by the charade, charges were not filed. The two American students left the college shortly after."

∾

Mercedes leaned back in her chair. *Okay, where will I go from here,* she thought. Sitting forward, she typed in the words, "Secretaries of World War II in Italy and Germany." There before her popped up a list of names, only these were not names one would think of as a secretary. She needed to find out more about the relationship between the secretaries of state of Germany and Italy. The article went on to tell the story of the defeat of the Italian and German troops. Not much else was written, only old history of the war.

Mercedes then typed the names "Alexia Boardenbach" and "Francine Audincourt." To her surprise, a clip from the *New York Times* appeared. The headline announced, "US Students Missing in Italy." The story below read, "Two college students, Alexia Boardenbach of Pedeaux, Ohio, and

THE *House* ON THE CORNER

Francine Audincourt of New Town, Ohio, disappeared while riding in an automobile. The two girls were on their way to Rome, Italy, to board a plane bound for the United States as reported by the parents of Alexia Boardenbach. When they didn't arrive at their scheduled time, a call was made by Miss Boardenbach and Miss Audincourt's parents to the United States Consulate, where they reported the girls missing. Authorities could not find any trace of the young women. Authorities are still investigating their disappearance." Mercedes continued to search through other search engines, but not finding anything else, she turned off the computer and headed for bed.

As she crawled into bed, the glow from the nightlight cast a dim shadow on the ceiling. Looking up at the ceiling, she noticed the ceiling tiles were not geometrically correct. In fact, the two tiles that would be in the middle of her bed were completely ostentatious. The rest of the ceiling tiles had small, intricate holes randomly scattered across their faces where in the two different tiles, the holes had the designs of small butterflies. These also appeared to be older than the rest of the tiles.

Getting her second wind, Mercedes got up and pushed the bed over. She went downstairs, got a step ladder, brought it up into the bedroom, and climbed up to within reach of the ceiling tiles. As Mercedes pushed up on the tiles, dust

The Meeting

bunnies fell into her face. Brushing her face, she peered into the ceiling. Unable to see in the darkness, she climbed back down, grabbed her flashlight from the nightstand drawer, and climbed back up the ladder. Turning the flashlight on, she saw two shoebox-sized metal boxes about four feet from where she was standing. Mercedes made another trip down the ladder. This time she got one of the wire hangers from the closet. Twisting the end of the hanger, she made a hook out of the end of the hanger.

Mercedes took the hanger back up the ladder and tried to find something on the box to grab onto with her hook. She finally caught the clasp of the first box and scooted it across the ceiling to where she was. As she pulled the metal box out of the ceiling, she almost dropped it to the floor as it was much heavier than it appeared. She climbed down the ladder and sat the box on the floor. Going back up the ladder she did the same thing and reached out toward the second box with the hanger. Again she found the clasp on the metal box and scooted this one across the floor as well. Pulling this box was easier as she thought it might be as heavy as the other, and true to her thinking, it was. Climbing down the ladder, she sat the second box on the floor beside the other one.

Mercedes went back up the ladder and reset the odd tiles where she'd found them. Then she climbed down, folded the ladder, took it back downstairs, put it away, and went back up

THE House ON THE CORNER

to her bedroom. Looking up again at the ceiling, she began to wonder if any other tiles in the other rooms were like this, but first she thought, *I'm putting my bed back, and then I'll see what the other ceilings look like in the morning.* Right now, she wanted to find out what was in the boxes.

After pulling the bedroom back in order, Mercedes turned off the light on the nightstand and turned on the overhead bedroom light. Picking up the first box, she dusted it and looked for the clasp to open the box. Both boxes were Army green; one had the stamp of the US Army on it with numbers stamped on the side. The clasp was metal with a small combination lock. The different thing about the box was besides the words "Property of the US Army" was the stamp of the flag of Germany instead of a stamp of the flag of the United States.

Mercedes looked around the room for something to use to try to pry the box open. Not finding anything suitable, she went back downstairs to her junk drawer in the kitchen and took out two screwdrivers, one a Phillips head screwdriver and one a flathead screwdriver, thinking she could possibly unscrew the hinge screws holding the box together. Just as she was about to turn around to go back upstairs, she heard the doorknob on the kitchen door move.

Mercedes turned around slowly and began backing toward the hallway to the stairs and noticed the shadowy

The Meeting

figure of a man at the door. As she moved toward the hallway, the man at the door continued to jiggle the doorknob as he tried to push the door open. She could hear him pushing and pushing on the door. Trying not to be afraid, she ran up the stairs, pushed the boxes under her bed, turned off the light, and called the police.

The police came with full lights and sirens. Mercedes could hear glass breaking and someone yelling. Upon hearing this, she locked her bedroom door and waited. After what seemed like an eternity, she heard footsteps on the stairs and someone knocking on her bedroom door. "Miss Adler, Miss Adler, are you all right in there?" a male voice asked excitedly.

Gingerly opening the door, Mercedes stood face-to-face with the tallest police officer she had ever seen. "Yes" she said. "Did you catch who was trying to break in?"

"Well, miss, it appears the person trying to get in to your home was someone we've seen around town for a while. He's sort of a loner, always walking around town, going through the dumpsters, looking for cans or something he can sell. He doesn't hold a steady job; doubt he's had one his whole life. His name is Ray Laroche. They call him Roachbug. We always thought he was harmless till tonight. Can we go downstairs? I'd like you to talk with my sergeant," the police office said.

THE *House* ON THE CORNER

Mercedes grabbed her robe and went downstairs with the policeman. When she walked into her kitchen, she noticed the glass in the kitchen door was broken. Seeing this and the man who was trying to get in now sitting at her kitchen table in handcuffs, she began to shake.

Donald Barnstool, sergeant of the Pedeaux Police Department, stood up, walked over to Mercedes, and said, "Miss Adler, are you acquainted with this man?" Mercedes shook her head no. "Then tell me something, Ray," the sergeant asked the man in handcuffs, "just what were you trying to do here tonight, scare this lady, break in the house, or what?"

"I don't have to tell you anything, you *pig!*" Ray Laroche shouted. "This place was my home long before she moved here. I've got stuff in the basement. She's got the door padlocked and I can't get into the basement to get my stuff. I just came by to get it. How would I know she'd locked the place up tighter than Fort Knox?"

Mercedes looked at him. "Mr. Laroche, there is absolutely nothing in the basement that belongs to you. When I moved in here everything was pretty well cleaned out. Anything in the basement that was trash was taken to the dump."

Ray Laroche started to stand, only to be pushed down by the policeman standing behind him. "You bitch!" he yelled. "I had valuables hidden down there. No one knew about them but me. You threw out all of the boxes that were in the corner of the back room?"

"It's all gone, all of it. There is nothing left down there, only things that belong to me. All you had to do was ask, Mr. Laroche, and you wouldn't be in this mess," said Mercedes.

Ray Laroche turned white as a sheet. "He'll be mad, so mad. I told him I knew where the stuff was. I had hidden it myself and he was gonna give me money for it. Enough money that I could leave this God-forsaken town and start a new life and you had to throw it away." He looked as if he could cry. "You don't know what it's like to have everyone laugh at you, point at you, and make noises when you walk by. I walk around this town every day. I start early in the morning and don't stop until late at night. I make more picking up other people's trash than most people make in a month. Now I'll never get out of here. And when he finds out, I'm just as good as dead."

"We're going to take you down to the station, Ray," said the sergeant. "Miss Adler, if you want to press charges for attempted breaking and entering, you can come down in the morning. Mr. Laroche will be a guest of the city for a while. I'm sure we can take good care of him."

Mercedes agreed to come to the station later that morning. She didn't go back to bed after they left though. Instead, she

THE House ON THE CORNER

took a shower, got dressed, and went back to work on the two metal boxes.

She didn't know why she wasn't upset about the attempted breaking and entering. She wasn't even worried about it. She was too excited to think about it. She found a scrap of plywood in the basement and quickly tacked it over the broken backdoor window as well as she could manage it. Mercedes wanted only to get the boxes open. Hopefully, the answers would be there to tell her exactly why the recent events happened and why the Pedosta boys were killed.

Before Mercedes went back upstairs, she again went to the junk drawer and took out a hammer. Going back upstairs, she stopped just long enough at the first landing of the stairs to look out the window. Standing on the corner was a man dressed in a red plaid shirt and blue jeans with an Ohio State ball cap looking at her house. Mercedes stepped back from the window and moved to the corner of the wall. She opened the curtain from just around the window facing. When she looked out the man on the corner was walking across the street to the hotel. As she watched, he disappeared into the hotel.

Mercedes went back into her bedroom, pulled the two metal boxes from under her bed, and began working on the lock of the first box. Seeing the screws in each corner were for a flathead screwdriver, Mercedes pulled the screwdriver off the nightstand and began working on them.

The Meeting

The screws were rusted solid in the metal box, and no amount of trying was going to turn them. Getting frustrated, she took the screwdriver and placed it in the shackle of the lock that went through the hasp locking the box and pounded on it until finally the lock popped open. Before opening the box, she did the same thing to the next box.

Opening the first box, she found two passports, one with the name Alexia Boardenbach and the other with the name Francine Audincourt. Mercedes studied the passports. Both women were beautiful. Alexia had long blonde hair. The passport photos were black-and-white, so there was no way to see what color her eyes were. The only clue was what was written on the passport. Francine had long dark hair. Mercedes was surprised the passports had come back to the United States with both women still missing. Mercedes planned to go back to the library after she went to the police station to see if she could find out if any reports of their being found had ever been printed.

Getting back to the box, Mercedes found a few pieces of jewelry, a crucifix, and a Bible. Mercedes read the inscription on the front page: "To our beautiful Alexia, you are the delight of the Sisters of St. Simenon. Good luck in finding your dreams when you go to college. Keep your prayers and say your Rosary and may God always be with you." Feeling around the inside of the box with her hand, Mercedes found a false bottom. Pushing gingerly on the bottom, it opened and a small butterfly fell into her hand. Holding the tiny object up to the light, she could see numbers written around the wings. Mercedes laid the butterfly in the middle of the Bible and opened the other box.

Inside this box were papers from the Bank of New York. Mercedes could feel her heart pounding. She laid the papers out. They appeared to be some sort of bonds written in Italian. Not knowing what they were, she decided she should put them in a safe place until she could find out for sure if they were anything important. She decided to take the contents of both boxes to the bank in the morning and put them in her own safety deposit box. Like the first box, there were more pieces of jewelry, but this time she found a book titled *Butterflies of the Western Hemisphere*. The copyright was dated 1942. She thumbed through the book and was about to put it down when she noticed the back of the book looked a little funny. Running her finger across the top and side of the back cover of the book, she found a place where it appeared the back of the book had been cut. She poked her finger in it and felt a piece of paper. Not wanting to damage the book and whatever was inside it, she put the book down carefully and got up and went to the medicine cabinet in the bathroom, took out a pair of tweezers, and went back to the bedroom.

The Meeting

Placing the tweezers in the book, she gently pulled the paper out. To her surprise, there was a page from a bank notepad with the words "Bank of New York" printed on top with the address of 1220 E. 95th St., New York, New York. Someone had written the words "lockbox 551, combination: 5 turns to the right to zero; 3 turns to the left back to zero; 2 turns to the right back to zero; then open."

Mercedes immediately put the paper back into the secret pocket cut in the binding of the butterfly book where she'd found it. She took the jewelry, passports, bonds, and the Bible and put them all in her backpack and placed it in her cedar chest and locked it. She didn't want to take the chance that someone might come in if she were in the shower and find what she had found. She pushed the two metal boxes back under the bed.

Picking up her tools and tidying up the mess she'd made as quickly as she could, Mercedes took everything downstairs. The sun was just starting to come up. As the coffee maker began to deliver her morning coffee, her cell phone started ringing. Picking it up, she heard an unfamiliar voice on the other end. "Mercedes, this is Dr. James Brock. I am a friend of Dr. Lajonque. He was called out of town on an emergency and wanted me to let you know if you needed anything you can just call me."

THE House ON THE CORNER

"Really?" said Mercedes. "What happened? Do you know when he'll be back?"

Dr. Brock hesitated, then said, "Uh, no, he didn't give me a date. Just said to watch out for you and to let you know that if you needed anything to call me. I didn't ask any questions as I just thought he was talking about fixing your house if something needed fixing or finding someone to do it or helping you with your car or something like that. Is there more that I should know?"

"No," said Mercedes. "It was kind of Dr. Lajonque to look out for me, but I think I'll be fine. I have your number on my phone, so if there is anything I need, I'll be happy to call you. Thank you for letting me know. We'll keep in touch, and by the way, if you talk with Dr. Lajonque, ask him to call me when he's free. I have some news about the horse he wanted me to look at. I'm pretty excited about her. Tell him her name is Franlexia's Dream. I'm sure he'll be impressed."

Mercedes clicked the button on the cell phone, ending the call there. Going over to the cupboard, she took out a coffee mug and poured the hot black liquid into the cup. She loved to smell coffee brewing, especially in the early morning hours. Sitting down at the table, she sipped the coffee and stared into space. She was thinking about all the events that had taken place over the past weeks when a knock on the door brought her back into the real world.

The Meeting

The space on the side of the curtain was just wide enough to see someone standing on the stoop, but Mercedes did not recognize the man standing there. He was tall, about six-four, dark hair with just a touch of gray at the temples, a permanent frown line between his eyebrows, and a mouth that looked as though he was never happy. He knocked on the door again, this time with a little more force.

Mercedes could tell from his body language he was getting tired of standing there, so she decided to wait a few more minutes. *Maybe, he'll just go away.* The stranger at the door pulled out an envelope and tried to put it under door. Not being successful, he stuck the envelope in the mailbox, turned around, went down the steps, and headed toward the tattoo parlor.

Mercedes slipped out and kept watching the door as she took the envelope out of the mailbox. Holding it up to the light, she could see there wasn't any type of paper in it, but she could tell there was writing on the inside of the envelope. Opening the envelope, the only words written inside were "8:00 p.m., fishing at Cornwall Lake."

God, thought Mercedes. *Here we go again, more cryptic messages.*

Mercedes went back upstairs, took a shower, dried off, got dressed, and headed down to the Second Chance bookstore. Here she would get lost for hours. She thought she might get

THE House ON THE CORNER

lucky enough to find an old book or two that belonged to any of the families she had just learned about.

The bookstore was quite different than any Mercedes had ever been in. Mercedes felt as though she'd walked into another world. One side of the bookstore was an antique shop where a little white-haired lady sat in a rocking chair rocking and knitting. She didn't even look up when Mercedes walked in. The middle part of the bookstore and the other side were lined with shelves and shelves of books. She noticed in what appeared to be a closet, shelf after shelf of books. All the books lining the shelves were nicely dusted, and each shelf was marked with the subject of the books on each section, whether it be "Fiction," "Nonfiction," "Historical," or whatever. Over in the corner was what appeared to be a self-service kiosk with a computerized cash register with a credit card machine sitting beside it.

Reading the titles of the books in the historical shelves, she found one about Pedeaux. Pulling it off the shelf, she looked through it only to find it was more modern than old world. She ended up putting it back on the shelf. As she continued skimming the book titles, she found another book titled *Murders in Pedeaux*. Intrigued by the title, she took it from the shelf and looked a little more. Not seeing anything else of interest, Mercedes went to the cash register and stood waiting for the knitting lady to throw another stitch

The Meeting

or two. When it appeared she wasn't going to stop, Mercedes started to leave the money on the counter. Her concentration ruined, the knitting lady said, "Do you have the right change?" Mercedes nodded her heard yes. "Then you can just take your book and leave. Next time, Miss Star should be here, and she'll be able to assist you if you're looking for something special. I'm just here to open the store and kinda keep an eye on it. Most people use the honor system and it works out well. No one has shorted us yet or stolen anything."

Mercedes thanked her and walked out the door with the book in her hand. She decided to go over to the coffee shop for a cappuccino and a croissant. Just as she was waiting to cross the street, she saw Dr. Lajonque's vehicle go by with Dr. Lajonque and the sheriff inside it. Not understanding what was going on, Mercedes took out her cell phone to see if it had somehow gotten on "silent." The ringer setting was still on "loud," so she knew Dr. Lajonque had not called her. She decided to forego the cappuccino and croissant and go back to her house. She would wait there until Dr. Lajonque called, *if he called*, she thought. She did know one thing. Something was definitely going on, and she planned on finding out what it was.

Mercedes had just walked through the door and put her things down on the counter when her phone started ringing. She picked it up and looked at the Caller ID. Seeing it was

THE *House* ON THE CORNER

Dr. Lajonque, she answered, "Hello, Dr. Lajonque, how's your day going?" Ignoring her attempt at polite conversation, Dr. Lajonque, sounding relieved to find Mercedes at home, said he would be at her house around two o'clock. He told her not to leave and to make sure she kept the doors and windows locked. He asked Mercedes where her car was, and she explained the car was in the lot behind the house and no, she hadn't looked to make sure it was there, but she would go right then. Dr. Lajonque told her to stay in the house; he would explain it all when he got there. All he would tell Mercedes was her car was found on an abandoned road. Inside was the body of Ray LaRoche. He'd been stabbed in the chest; his legs were tied together with baling twine, and the fingernails on his hands were painted red. After telling her he would talk with her later, Dr. Lajonque ended the call, and Mercedes turned off the phone. Sitting on the stool, she laid the phone on the bar and stared into space. The thoughts running through her mind were a blur. In just the past week, there had been at least three new murders she knew about and rumors of others, there had been two mysterious disappearances, a skeleton in her basement, and a rotating cast of dark cars parked across from her house. She was feeling nauseated. She headed upstairs to the bedroom. She thought if she were able to lie down for a few hours, this feeling would

The Meeting

go away, and she would be fine. Mercedes made it to her room, took off her shoes, and lay on the quilt and fell asleep.

In the meantime, Dr. Lajonque was riding in a cruiser with the sheriff on their way to the crime scene where Ray LaRoche's body had been found in a car that belonged to Mercedes. There were a lot of questions to be answered. Dr. Lajonque was hoping whoever found the car and Ray LaRoche would have some of the answers.

The driver of the cruiser was Sheriff Tommy Darnt. He had just passed the lieutenants' exam the first year out of college. The adrenaline was pumping through his body like it did when he'd played football for the Pedeaux High School Knights. Always trying to run faster than any of the other boys, Tommy's large six foot, seven inch frame that weighed in at two hundred and ninety pounds was all legs and arms. He never mastered the coordination needed for running, but he did master the ability to wrestle and became a state champion in the 295-pound weight class. No one had beaten him. He had been offered full-ride scholarships to Harvard and Yale, not just because of his athletic ability but his academics as well. He was first in a class of 312. He carried straight A's throughout his elementary, middle school, and high school years, but he turned the Ivy League down to go to college in his hometown where he would double major in criminal psychology and forensic science with a minor in English literature.

THE *House* ON THE CORNER

Sheriff Darnt graduated from Ashball College suma cum laude with a perfect 4.0 average. He was being courted by the television show Wrestling Stars of America (WSA) to wrestle the next champion. Turning the six-figure offer down, he chose to follow his dream of becoming the next sheriff of Parson County when Vernon Jeffries, the current sheriff, retired. Having no intention of trying to root him out or play the internal political game of undermining the sheriff, he would learn all he could from this man who had been like a father to him after his own father had passed away from Lou Gehrig's disease, also known as ALS, a very cruel and debilitating disease that leaves the person virtually a prisoner in their bodies until eventually the only thing that they have any control of is their eyes. All the other muscles eventually atrophy until the heart finally stops.

Sheriff Darnt was fourteen when his father died. His father had been a farmer who was also a township trustee. He was very well-respected in the county and was well-known for his sense of humor and his love for the people he served in Parson County. All this he'd taught to Tommy. He and Vernon had been friends since boyhood, and when Tommy's dad finally passed away and his mother decided to return to her own family in Virginia, Vernon took the boy in. His mother, Kathrine ("Kat") Edwins, was a professor at Brighton University in Virginia where she'd taught English

The Meeting

literature before marrying Tommy's dad and moving to the farm. She'd refused to take her husband's name when they married. Always the quiet feminist, she firmly believed in the right to choose whatever path you wanted to take in life. About twice a year—Christmas and Easter—you would see Kat in town to visit Tommy. She stopped offering to bring Tommy to Virginia after he made his dream job known. During the Tommy's first year as lieutenant, Sheriff Vernon Jeffries passed away from a massive heart attack. The funeral was attended by several hundred police officers, sheriff's deputies, and highway patrol officers from around the state. Since the sheriff had never married, his estate would be left to Tommy, which included the sheriff's house and his personal vehicles.

At first, Tommy wasn't sure what to do with his inheritance. He contacted his mother for advice. She took care of everything for Tommy. After the dust settled, the Compton County commissioners appointed Tommy to finish the unexpired term of Sheriff Jeffries, after which Tommy was elected to the term by popular vote.

Rounding the curve, Tommy and Dr. Lajonque could see the lights of the emergency vehicles, police cars, and other vehicles. Tommy stopped the cruiser next to the ambulance. The coroner was leaning against the car and writing on a pad. His glasses were on top of his head (the usual place he would

THE House ON THE CORNER

leave them and spend countless minutes looking for them as he would forget he put them up there). Tommy and Dr. Lajonque got out of the car. Dr. Lajonque wasn't really sure why Tommy had asked him to come, only he knew he wanted to be there to find out just why this man found it necessary to be found dead in Mercedes's car.

Dr. Lajonque looked into the vehicle. Ray LaRoche was sitting behind the steering wheel. His eyes were open. There was a small bit of blood running down his neck from a tiny hole just below his left earlobe. It looked like the kind of mark a needle would leave.

Dr. Lajonque backed away from the car. Better to leave the crime scene untouched by his hands. He thought Mercedes must be getting too close to the real reason all the three previous murders had taken place, or at least whoever did these murders thought she was too close. He decided to talk with the sheriff and bring him up to speed as to what Mercedes and he had found out so far. Maybe the sheriff or the police chief would assign one of their deputies or policemen to watch to make sure no one bothered her. He would have to make sure she didn't know she had protection.

Sheriff Darnt walked around the car looking for any signs of damage. The car looked fine. Hopefully there would be some fingerprints, signs of a struggle, or something that would lead them to what had taken place. As he was standing there thinking, one of the EMTs walked over to the sheriff. "Looks like he may have had a heart attack. We didn't find any type of weapons lying around. The footprints around the car are smudged at best. We really won't know anything until the autopsy, so we can't rule anything out," she stated.

The sheriff thought for a minute, nodded, and turned to one of his deputies, Brian Russo, and said, "Go ahead and let the coroner know he can get him out of here, and have the car towed to the county garage. We need to go over it for prints and see if anything else is inside the car." Pausing for a moment, Sheriff Darnt said, "Be sure to call Miss Adler and tell her we are impounding her car and she will get it back when we are finished."

The ambulance took Ray LaRoche's body to the county morgue. Deputy Russo called Tony's Towing to retrieve Mercedes's automobile. They were to take it to the Compton County Highway Garage for further investigation.

When Sheriff Darnt and Dr. Lajonque got back in the sheriff's cruiser and headed for the county morgue, Sheriff Darnt radioed his office and told the dispatcher to run a check on Ray LaRoche to see if there were any outstanding warrants or if he had been arrested at any time recently. He instructed his assistant to put any and all information on his desk before he got back. In the meantime, he was going to Ray LaRoche's house to take a look around there.

THE *House* ON THE CORNER

Fifteen minutes later they sat in the driveway of Ray LaRoche's home. What was surprising was how close it was to Mercedes's home. Getting out of the cruiser, they walked up the steps to the front porch and knocked. No one came to the door. They peered through the sidelight window of the door, and it looked as though no one had lived in that house for a very long time. What furniture they could see was dusty, and the mantle behind the chair looked just as bad. Above the mantle was a picture of a man and woman.

Sheriff Darnt was the first to speak. "Looks like no one has lived here for quite some time. Wonder how long this guy has been here. Better go get a search warrant before we take our little look see 'cause he may have relatives or such who might come here, and I don't want to be in here without it."

Dr. Lajonque nodded his agreement. Sheriff Darnt got on his cell phone and called the district attorney's office and explained why they needed the search warrant to follow up on the death of Ray LaRoche. He told the clerk to make sure it stated the sheriff's office had full access to the entire premises, which would include the house, garage, attic, and basement, as well as any outbuildings on the premises. Finally, he instructed the clerk to have one of the deputies bring the warrant to them out at Ray's place as soon as possible. He would be waiting in the cruiser.

The Meeting

Deputy Karl Smith arrived about fifteen minutes later with the requested search warrant. Getting out of the cruiser, Sheriff Darnt and Dr. Lajonque walked up the steps a second time. Dr. Lajonque turned the knob on the door and was surprised to find it turned very easily to the point of the door opening into the living room.

Walking into the room, they found the cushions on the sofa were as dusty as the end tables. The overstuffed easy chair had mouse droppings in the corner of the cushion, and the skirting around the chair was starting to fray.

As they walked through to the hallway, Dr. Lajonque was surprised to see the condition of the oil paintings hanging on the walls. The paintings here appeared to be clean. There was no dust on the frames or on the paintings themselves. *How odd*, he thought. Most of the paintings were landscapes depicting mountains and rivers.

Some were fox hunting themes. He knew Mercedes would love those.

As Dr. Lajonque got near the end of the hall, he stopped and looked into what appeared to be the library. This room was clean. There was no dust in the room; all the shelves were clean, as was the furniture. As he started to walk toward the desk, he noticed a paper lying on the floor. Picking it up, he noticed the words on the paper were written in script writing. It said, "Here lies the body of Rodney, a good old chap he could be, lost to the beauty of a precious young thing, who always made his heart ring. When walking through the field, checking the corn." The poem or sonnet ended without any more written.

Dr. Lajonque folded the paper and placed it in his billfold. He would give it to the sheriff for processing later.

Continuing to look around, they decided this must be the room where Ray spent most of his time. The books were clean. Built just below the bay window was a seat with a cushion on top. Noticing the latch in the middle just below the cushion, Dr. Lajonque lifted the cushion and the seat to find a storage area packed full of books. Taking them out one by one, he found they were all books about anatomy, surgical procedures, how to set up an operating room, dissecting organs and tissue, as well as various journals with notes and writings about suicides that had taken place in Europe and the United States between 1942 up to present day.

Dr. Lajonque put the books back where he had found them. He would be sure to let the sheriff know he had taken them out as his prints were now on the books. Looking around the room, something about the wall behind Ray's desk seemed odd. As he approached the wall, he could see the paneling on the wall was two different colors, and the seams were off. It appeared to be two different types of paneling.

One was smooth with a dark finish, and the other was the rough type, although it too was dark like the other.

    Running his fingers down the seam, Dr. Lajonque hit a slight dip in this seam. About the time his fingers touched the seam, the whole wall started to move. The paneling Dr. Lajonque had touched slid behind the other panel. There was a shelf built into the wall behind the paneling. On the shelf were two photo albums with the words "Pedostifino a.k.a. Pedosta" embossed on the covers. Dr. Lajonque took the top album and, turning around and sitting down in the desk chair, he laid this album on the desk. Opening to the first page, he found a picture of a house with "Home, 1942" written under it. As he flipped through the album, Dr. Lajonque could see dozens of pictures of different towns, landscapes, homes, and sunsets. There were no pictures of family or friends. Closing this album, he turned to take out the second one. The same words were written on this one, only the words "Volume II" were added. Opening this book, he found a picture of a young Mary Pedosta. She was sitting on the grass with the sunlight shining on her head, making her black hair look almost blue. She looked happy facing the camera with a big smile and dark eyes. On the back of the picture was written, "Mary, always smiling, always happy, always the love of my life." The signature was faded. *This will be something for the writing experts to decipher*, Dr. Lajonque thought.

THE *House* ON THE CORNER

While the sheriff and Dr. Lajonque were across town trying to find out what caused the death of Ray LaRoche, Mercedes woke from her nap. Looking at the clock, she saw she had been asleep for about five hours. Putting her shoes on, she looked on the nightstand for her cell phone. She thought she'd left it there; in fact, she remembered bringing it upstairs and plugging it in the charger. She looked behind the nightstand, under the bed, and behind the headboard. There was no sign of the phone or the charger.

Going downstairs, Mercedes thought maybe she dreamt that she'd brought the phone and charger upstairs. She didn't notice the daylight was almost gone and nighttime was coming on fast. As she started into the kitchen, something on the floor caught her eye. There on the floor laid her cell phone. Picking it up, Mercedes thought she must have dropped it on her way upstairs. Looking for the charger, she found it lying on the floor around the kitchen cabinets. As she bent down to pick up the charger, something fell from the counter and hit her in the head. Falling to her knees, she immediately felt sick to her stomach. She became dizzy, disoriented, and thought she saw someone in front of her. She thought it was a man. And that was the last thing she saw as she passed out on the floor.

How long she'd lain on the floor, no one could say. When Dr. Lajonque called Mercedes and she didn't answer her phone, he became concerned. He called again and still no answer. He knew she hadn't gone out—someone had stolen her auto—and he'd called her and warned her to stay home.

Dr. Lajonque found Sheriff Darnt and shared his concerns regarding Mercedes not answering her phone. Feeling like something was wrong, Sheriff Darnt told Dr. Lajonque to get in his cruiser; they would head over to Mercedes's house and check on her. The Sheriff called dispatch and gave instructions to send an unmarked police car to 100 W. Main Street right away—a wellness check on the resident. They were to report the findings as soon as possible.

Leaving the crime scene, the sheriff and Dr. Lajonque headed toward downtown and Mercedes's house. When they arrived at her home, an ambulance was just pulling into the driveway behind the house. Fearing the worst, Dr. Lajonque jumped out of the cruiser before the sheriff had gotten it into Park. Running into the house, he found the paramedics leaning over Mercedes. Dr. Lajonque stood back; he knew the paramedics would do everything they could for her. When he saw her head start to move toward the paramedic, relief swept over him as he had feared the worst.

"Is she all right?" he asked.

"Not sure, Doc. Looks like the bump on top of her head is going to cause her one hell of a headache," one of the paramedics replied.

THE *House* ON THE CORNER

"Think we need to take her to the hospital for observation, and one of the docs on duty will talk with her after they've examined her," the other one said.

As the paramedics loaded Mercedes into the ambulance, Dr. Lajonque looked around at the crowd that had started to gather to watch what was going on. This put him in mind of a time when he was a young boy. The neighbor lady had died of a stroke, and the fire department's rescue squad was called to take care of her. Of course, no one knew she had died from the stroke until after the autopsy. Most people thought she had just died of old age. After all, she was a whopping eighty-eight years old, so most folks just figured she had outlived her usefulness and the only reason they performed the autopsy was because of a selfish son who had lived with her up until the day she died. Rumor had it, once the old girl had been laid to rest and her estate was settled, the selfish son had to share the inheritance with his younger sister whom he did not like or trust.

Putting these thoughts away, Dr. Lajonque got in the ambulance with Mercedes, while Sheriff Darnt stayed at the scene to assist the Pedeaux PD in trying to solve the assault on Mercedes Adler. Arriving at the hospital, Mercedes was whisked into an exam room with Dr. Lajonque not far behind. As quickly as he went into the room, he was just as quickly escorted back out by a very prim and proper nurse

The Meeting

who could have passed for an Army sergeant in her heyday. She informed Dr. Lajonque they would come and get him or the doctor would come out and talk with him after they had completed their examinations.

Sitting for what seemed like forever in the waiting area, Dr. Lajonque noticed the people sitting around him. There on the sofa sat a young couple. The woman was definitely pregnant, and she looked like she would deliver about any time, while across the way the woman sitting next to the older man just kept wringing her hands in worry. Down the hall a young man sat near the entrance doors. It was as if he was waiting for someone. Dr. Lajonque started watching the young man. The young man stood up and walked across the hall to a vending machine. After he put some coins in the machine, Dr. Lajonque heard the sound of a candy bar falling into the tray where you pick it up. Dr. Lajonque thought this young man looked like someone he had seen before. As he watched the young man and tried to place him in memory, Dr. Straw, the Adler family's physician, came into the hospital.

She looked at Dr. Lajonque, nodded, and started for the examination room. Dr. Lajonque caught her by her arm and turned her around. "Okay, Doc, what's the scoop?" he asked. Dr. Straw hesitated, then said, "I got a call from the emergency room doctor. She said Mercedes has had a concussion, but that's not the bad part. Evidently, whoever hit her in the head wasn't content on just busting her skull; he tried to slit her throat but didn't get the job finished because he only put a three inch gash in her neck. If he had moved the knife one more inch, he would have hit her jugular vein and that would have ended her life. Something happened to make him stop. This we can be thankful for. What I need to do now is find out how badly injured she really is and what damage has been done to her throat. As soon as I get any information, I'll come and get you. Go on into the doctor's lounge and get some coffee. I believe there's something to eat there too. Some of the cooks make a snack for us to get us through the night. I'll be out as soon as I can. Don't worry, Gerald, we'll take good care of her."

Dr. Lajonque watched her walk away and turned and started down the hall to the doctors' lounge. His mind wandered back to the first time he met Mercedes Adler. *What a spitfire she was!* He would watch her bring that Airedale puppy into his office. She would sit in the waiting room and let everyone who came in with their dog, puppy, piggy, kitten, snake, rabbit, or hedgehog go before her. She would laugh when it finally got to the point the office girl would threaten to start charging her rent if she didn't take her turn. When Dr. Lajonque asked her why she'd waited so long, she smiled and told him it was the only time "D. K." (whose registered name was Adlers Danny Kaye) could socialize with other animals.

The Meeting

D. K. was born with a congenital kidney disease. Mercedes didn't believe this was true, so she took him to Ostenwatch University Animal Hospital where they would find the same diagnosis as did Dr. Lajonque. Later, she read in an article that in California there was a university that was performing experimental kidney transplants on dogs with congenital kidney disease like D. K. had. They would take a healthy kidney from a donor dog. Calling the operator, Mercedes got the number for the university animal clinic and had the opportunity to speak with one of the doctors performing the research. Mercedes asked if the kidney from the donor dog had to be a match and was told no. The greater problem was with the diseased dogs' bodies rejecting the donor kidneys. Asking where the donor dogs came from, Mercedes was surprised to learn they were "pound dogs," dogs that had been taken off the street or run away from their forever home or had been surrendered to the pound because their owners had moved, died, or could no longer afford them, or they had just dumped them. If D. K. were a candidate for the surgery, Mercedes would have to sign a contract agreeing to leave D. K. at the hospital for at least ten days, and when he was ready to go home, she'd take the donor dog as well, meaning she would have to adopt the donor dog in order to save D. K. She decided to wait until there were more published findings before she would put D. K. through this. She had discussed this with Dr. Lajonque, who agreed she was making the right decision. He promised her if he received any additional information about the study, he would share it with her. To expand his social horizons, Mercedes decided to take D. K. to visit the elderly residents at a local nursing home, where D. K. became the hit of the nursing home. Sadly, D. K. passed away shortly after beginning his career as a service dog.

For a long time, Mercedes wouldn't even look at the dogs in the pet stores at the malls. Finally, Dr. Lajonque brought her a silky terrier. She was two years old and weighed only four pounds. She had been brought to Dr. Lajonque by the Silky Terrier Rescue group. A concerned citizen had called to report abuse being committed by his neighbor, especially by the neighbor's ten-year-old son. He would chase the little dog around the house and yard, always with a broom handle or pair of cap guns. The final straw came when the citizen witnessed the father of the boy pick up the dog and try to punt it across the yard after the dog soiled his precious lawn. It was this action that caused the citizen to call the rescue group.

CHAPTER 13

The Hospital

As soon as he saw the dog, Dr. Lajonque knew exactly the right person who could give her the kind of home she deserved. He called Mercedes and led her to believe he had too many small dogs in residence and he needed her to keep the dog for a few days. Protesting, she finally agreed. "But only for a few days, no more than a week," she said. When Dr. Lajonque brought the tiny, raggedy-looking dog to Mercedes, the look on her face told him he had made the right decision.

Taking the pitiful looking dog from him, she held her up with both hands and looked into her worried little face and asked, "What kind of dog is she?" Dr. Lajonque explained to her the dog was a silky terrier. When he weighed her, she'd weighed out at four pounds. He had given the dog a complete physical. It appeared she had tried to have puppies. From the looks of her, if she had carried the puppies to term it would have killed her. She had been kicked in the mouth, breaking a few of her teeth and leaving jagged pieces pushing into the gums, but those injuries were healing and Dr. Lajonque expected her to make a full recovery.

Mercedes kept stroking the dog. Looking at Dr. Lajonque, she told him she would name her Sadie Lauren Bacall Cook. Now she would have had "D. K. and Bacall." About six months later, Mercedes would adopt Sophia Loren Cook (Sophie), and finally, Daisy Mae Cook would arrive. Daisy Mae wasn't a silky terrier like Sadie and Sophie; she was a shih tzu. It would take three dogs to fill the void left by D. K. These little girls became companions for Mercedes. They would go everywhere she could take them.

Dr. Lajonque looked at his watch. Mercedes had been in the operating room three hours. *What is going on, and why isn't Dr. Straw coming out?* As he stood thinking, the doors to the operating room finally opened. Dr. Straw walked over to Dr. Lajonque. "Sit down, Gerald. You look like death warmed over. Mercedes is in the recovery room. She will be there for about an hour, then we're moving her to the intensive care unit. She has a trach to assist her breathing. I figure she'll be in intensive care for about a week. This is more precautionary than anything," Dr. Straw stated.

"Will she be able to talk?" asked Dr. Lajonque.

"In time, Gerald, in time. Right now, she needs plenty of rest with very few people talking to her. I'll let you see her, but only for a few minutes. Please don't try to get her to talk, just let her sleep," Dr. Straw said.

They walked into the recovery room where Mercedes was lying with her head turned just ever so slightly to the right. She had just enough tape around her throat to indicate there was a problem. A vent tube was sticking out of the hole in the tape covering her throat, helping her breathe. She was hooked to a ventilator that also was helping her breathe. Mercedes looked ashen. Gerald turned away with tears in his eyes. He was somewhat confused. *If her throat was cut like Dr. Straw said, then why was it necessary for them to put in a trach and have her on a respirator?* She wasn't paralyzed; her lungs weren't affected. There had to be more going on than Dr. Straw was willing to talk about. Dr. Lajonque made up his mind he would find out the next day.

Right now he wanted to go home and go to bed. He had a lot to think about. But first, he would make call to Sheriff Darnt to find out if he'd had any luck in finding out who had done this to Mercedes. He walked over to Mercedes and placed his hand on hers. She stirred and went back to the position she was in when he walked in the room. Dr. Lajonque leaned over and whispered something in her ear.

THE *House* ON THE CORNER

She didn't move, and he could tell she was still under the effects of the anesthesia.

When he was ready to leave, Dr. Lajonque found two sheriff's deputies were waiting at the door. One told him he was going to drive him back to his car, and the other one was going to stay and keep an eye on Mercedes with orders that the only people allowed in her room were medical personnel and law enforcement officials.

After he got his car, Dr. Lajonque drove over to Mercedes's house to look at the scene. He knew the sheriff had gone over everything with a fine-toothed comb, but something was eating at him. He decided it was time to find out if his hunch was right.

Pulling into the parking lot behind Mercedes's house, he looked around. Yellow crime scene tape was pulled around the sidewalk all the way up to the front door of Mercedes's house. Stooping under the crime scene tape, he climbed up the steps to her house, put his key in the door, turned the handle, and walked into the house. Everything looked the same as when he was there a couple of days before. He stood for a long time looking around. Something just wasn't right. He knew it but couldn't figure out what it was. Just as he started to turn and leave, he remembered what it was. Bounding up the stairs, he ran into Mercedes's bedroom. Looking under the bed, he saw the board on the floor with a sticker on it. It appeared to have fallen from a book or come from a yard sale.

Pushing the bed next to the wall, he walked over to the floor and bent down. Placing his index finger on the end of the board with the sticker on it, he pushed down, and the other end of the board flipped up. Reaching into the space below, he found the book with the notes Mercedes was keeping since she had first come to town. He decided to take the notebook to the bank and place it in his own safety deposit box until Mercedes was well enough to come home. Putting the notebook in a laptop case that was lying on a chest, he moved the board back to its original place and moved the bed back over it.

Feeling relieved and thankful Mercedes had told him about the hiding place, he picked up the laptop case and headed for the stairs. Listening intently, he walked down the stairs. Just as he got to the last step, he saw a shadow at the front door. Waiting, he saw the doorknob turn. The person at the door started knocking. When no one answered, the person at the door slipped an envelope under the door and left.

Dr. Lajonque walked over to the door and picked up the envelope off the floor. It was addressed to Mercedes without a return address. The envelope was dirty. Placing the envelope on the countertop, Dr. Lajonque took a pen from the inside pocket of his jacket. He placed the pen into a corner of the envelope. He then walked into the bathroom and turned on the light. Holding the envelope in the light, he tried to make out the words on the paper inside the envelope, but the paper showed smears and stains, and the letters appeared to be mixed up in the stains and smears. He put the pen and the envelope in the inside pocket of his jacket.

Making sure the lights were turned off with the exception of the night lights, and turning on the burglar alarm, Dr. Lajonque stepped out the door. Moving the crime scene tape, he placed it back on the brick, turned around, and started walking toward his truck, which he'd parked behind Mercedes's house.

There, behind the house, beside Dr. Lajonque's truck, stood a very large man. Looking at Dr. Lajonque, then looking at the laptop case, he started toward Dr. Lajonque. Dr. Lajonque stood his ground as the man kept getting closer.

As the man got close enough for Dr. Lajonque to see his face, the man turned abruptly and walked away. Still standing and watching the man walk away, Dr. Lajonque tried to remember the man and his face: the mouth that seemed somewhat pulled to the right, hands big enough to choke the life out of a person in just a few seconds, and dark eyes set close together. His forehead was wide with high cheekbones divided by a very large roman nose set above two very wide lips. As the man got near the corner, he turned and said to Dr. Lajonque, "Watch your step, Doc. You might be next!" He then disappeared into the night.

Dr. Lajonque was visibly shaken by the altercation. He would have to make sure he told the sheriff, and he would definitely be able to give them a proper description of the perpetrator. Driving home, he dialed the hospital to check on Mercedes. But even after explaining to the nurse on duty who he was, the nurse held her ground and said she could not give him any information due to HIPAA. Hearing this, he turned the truck at the next corner and headed for the hospital.

He parked in the hospital lot and walked into the lobby in the direction of the elevators. Sitting near the elevator was Harper Pedosta. She was talking on her cell phone. As Dr. Lajonque approached her, he could hear that she was speaking in French. As she looked up and saw him walking toward her, she quickly ended her conversation, stood up, and walked toward him.

"Gerald, oh Gerald, what has happened to our Mercedes? I came here because someone left me a voice message saying Mercedes had been in an accident. She has no relatives to call to tell so they can come and be with her. I came but they won't give me any information. I am so worried. Please, tell them to talk with us and let us know what is going on," Harper Pedosta said.

THE *House* ON THE CORNER

Dr. Lajonque took Harper Pedosta's hand and said, "Don't worry, Harper. We will go up and see her now. She is in intensive care, so we won't be able to stay long. I think she will be pleased to know you thought enough of her to come."

Harper Pedosta nodded her head in agreement. Both were quiet, thinking their own thoughts as they walked to the elevator. Getting in the elevator, Dr. Lajonque pushed the button marked "intensive care unit" and, as before, stood silent.

When the doors opened, they walked to the nurses' station. The nurse knew Dr. Lajonque as he'd saved the life of her Cairn Terrier–Jack Russell cross.

She had bought the little fellow at a pet store called "Justagoodfriend." After getting him home, she thought he was acting strange. He would eat good for a few days but would stop eating for a few more days. When he became lethargic, she took him to see Dr. Lajonque. Dr. Lajonque knew what was wrong as soon as he checked the dog's gums. Taking a small amount of blood from the ailing puppy, he put a few drops on a slide and put it under the microscope. He put the rest of the blood in a vial, corked it, and put it in a machine that would run a full panel of tests for enzymes, iron deficiency, and a dozen other factors.

Sally Pathway, intensive care nurse at St. Jeramiah Hospital, sat in the waiting room wringing her hands. She was thinking everyone else could have a pet and all she ever wanted was a nice little dog to come home to. She had stopped in for a "quick looksee" at the puppies and fell immediately in love with the smallest puppy in the store. The sign said he was a Cairn Terrier–Jack Russell cross. She even thought of a name while holding him. She would call him "Jack." It didn't take any persuasion to sell the puppy to Sally. She did get a discount because he was the last of the litter and was the runt. Now, he was sick. *Oh, God*, she thought, *please don't let Jack die.*

Dr. Lajonque walked out of the examining room carrying a very energetic puppy named Jack. Looking around the waiting room, he said (much too loudly), "Is there anyone in this room who belongs to this little man?" Sally jumped up. She almost tripped over a sleeping English bulldog. When she got to Dr. Lajonque, she took the lively puppy from his hands.

Dr. Lajonque told Sally her puppy was still sick, but if she would make sure he took the medicine he was giving her, he would get better. The diagnosis was iron deficiency anemia as well as a calcium deficiency, which were caused from being taken away from his mother at a very young age. He probably wasn't even old enough to be weaned. It was surprising to Dr. Lajonque that the puppy had even lived. Asking Sally where she had bought the puppy, she very willingly gave him the card the pet store had given her. He would later become involved with the closing of the "Justagoodfriend" pet store. It was found the owners of the store had ties to the puppy mills operating around the tri-state area. They would get puppies aged four to six weeks old, barely big enough to be away from their mothers. If the puppies didn't sell before they were three months old, they were discounted. If they still didn't sell, the puppies were then sold to laboratories for research. As it would turn out, Dr. Lajonque and Sally Pathway would become advocates for the investigation, fining, and closing of the puppy mills and their owners.

Sally opened the door to Mercedes's room. A Pedeaux city policeman sat just inside the door, and a county sheriff's deputy sat on the other side of the room. At the ends of the hall were two state highway patrolman, and down in the lobby there were three plainclothes detectives.

Dr. Lajonque was thankful there was this much protection; he didn't know the reason Mercedes had been attacked, but he did know the person or persons who did this almost killed her, and he sure didn't want to leave the slightest chance for someone to come in the room and finish the job.

Harper Pedosta walked over to Mercedes and, taking Mercedes's hand and stroking it, said softly in French, *"le bouton de rose."* The look on Dr. Lajonque's face told Harper he didn't understand what she'd just said. Speaking to him she said, "Le bouton de rose" means 'rosebud, a bud.' I was telling her she was like a rosebud, frail and delicate."

Dr. Lajonque just smiled. Looking at Mercedes, he noticed her breathing seemed to be off. Taking her other hand into his, he started to say something to Harper Pedosta when Mercedes started convulsing.

Harper Pedosta hit the nurse's call button. Immediately, the nurse appeared and, taking her cell phone from her pocket, she hit a button. The intercom sounded, "Code green, room 325 STAT!" In what seemed like less than a minute, a whole team of nurses and doctors appeared. Harper Pedosta and Dr. Lajonque moved to the back of the room.

No one said anything, just focused on the tasks before them. After what seemed like forever, Mercedes was stable again, and the team left just as quickly as they'd come in. Only one doctor remained, Doctor Reynald Satchai.

Dr. Lajonque gave Dr. Satchai the once over. Dr. Satchai had moved to Pedeaux, Ohio, after completing her residency at the Silver City Memorial Hospital in Silver City, Ohio. Dr. Lajonque really didn't know a whole lot about her, only, as his secretary would tell him, the "important stuff."

He knew she wasn't married but was engaged to a doctor in Silver City who came to Pedeaux only on weekends. Rumor had it she wasn't interested in leaving Pedeaux, so if

THE *House* ON THE CORNER

this marriage was to work, then the good doctor from Silver City would have to move to Pedeaux.

Dr. Lajonque walked over to Dr. Satchai and asked her, "What caused the convulsions? Is she allergic to the medicine you're giving her, or is this from the head trauma?"

Dr. Satchai asked, "And who might you be?"

"I am one of two friends this young lady has. She has no living relatives to care for her. She just moved to Pedeaux a few weeks ago. Harper Pedosta and I, Dr. Gerald Lajonque, spend just about every day with her. Now, would you please tell me what is going on?"

"As you know, she has had a severe head trauma. Her brain is swelling as we speak. We are trying to stop the swelling so we can reduce the pressure on her brain, and we are watching her constantly. There will be a nurse checking on her every fifteen minutes. If anything changes, we will call you," Dr. Satchai stated in a very emphatic voice. Dr. Lajonque told Dr. Satchai he would be there until Mercedes was out of danger. He had no intention of leaving her at this time. Harper Pedosta agreed with Dr. Lajonque. She too would stay as there was something about this young woman she needed to know more about. Besides, the house Mercedes lived in belonged at one time to the Pedosta family. She would like to learn more about it, and now she had someone to help her find out some more about the "Pedosta roots."

The Hospital

Dr. Satchai left the room. A short time later, two maintenance men came into the room with two recliners. These would become Dr. Lajonque's and Harper Pedosta's beds for the duration. A nursing assistant brought in towels and an assortment of tiny bath soaps, shampoos, and deodorants. Anything else, they would have to supply for themselves.

Dr. Lajonque sat down in his chair and laid his head back against the headrest. In a few minutes, Harper Pedosta could see he had drifted off to sleep. She too sat down in the recliner, and like Dr. Lajonque, she drifted off to sleep.

Mercedes moved. When she did, every bone in her body seemed to ache. "Where am I?" she said out loud.

Dr. Lajonque woke with a start. He thought he'd heard Mercedes. Looking at her, he saw she was awake and looking right at him. Standing from the chair, he walked over to her bed and pushed the nurses' call button. "Hi, it's good to see you," he replied. Mercedes couldn't keep her eyes open. She kept drifting off to sleep. The doctor had said if she came out of it, she would be groggy, with some memory loss.

Mercedes woke again. When she did, she willed herself to stay awake. She wasn't sure where she was or how she got there. The last thing she remembered was talking to Dr. Lajonque. Now, she was in unfamiliar surroundings. It looked like a hospital room, maybe. Finally, she took the chance and looked over at Dr. Lajonque. *Who was that sitting with him?*

Dr. Lajonque was watching her. So was Harper Pedosta and someone else who Mercedes didn't know. *Was that a nurse? What is going on?*

Dr. Satchai spoke to Mercedes. "Hello, Mercedes. Do you know where you are?" she asked.

Mercedes tried to shake her head, and when she did, she felt an excruciating pain that ran from the top of her head down the left side of her face, through her neck to her chest. As fast as the pain hit, it left just as quickly.

Looking at Dr. Satchai, Mercedes opened her mouth and said, "Where am I, and how did I get here?" Watching Mercedes with the eyes of a skilled surgeon, Dr. Satchai answered by saying, "I think you just asked where you are and how you got here, is that correct?"

Mercedes didn't try to shake her head. She just looked at her.

"Mercedes, you were in an accident. You've been in a semi-comatose state for the past few days. You just woke up a few minutes ago. Do you remember anything at all about the accident?" Dr. Satchai asked.

Mercedes had to think hard. She couldn't figure out why these people had put a hospital bed into a hotel room. She had something on her head that felt tight. Now, this woman who she didn't know from Adam was asking her questions.

"Gerald," she said, "tell this woman I wasn't in an accident. I live in the country with my dogs and horses. Now, please get my clothes. While I'm getting dressed, have one of the bellhops bring my car around. I don't know your friend, but she can go ahead and leave as there's no more to see here."

Dr. Lajonque looked at Dr. Satchai. Dr. Satchai just shook her head as if to say, "Go along with her, we'll explain it later."

Harper Pedosta turned and walked to the door. She said to Mercedes, "When you are well, Mercedes, we will take a long trip to Paris and London. I will show you places that are not in the travel brochures. You will see beautiful landscapes and art like you've never been introduced to. Just get better, Mercedes, we will talk soon." With this, Harper Pedosta walked out the door.

"Do I know her?" asked Mercedes.

Dr. Lajonque walked over to Mercedes's bed. Sitting down on the side of the bed, he took her one of her hands into both of his, and smoothing her hand with his, he explained to her the events that put her in the hospital.

"How much time have I lost? Am I going to get my memory back? Who did this to me? Who hates me so much they want to hurt me, and just who is that woman with the funny voice?" a very angry and confused Mercedes asked.

Dr. Satchai spoke up. "Questions, questions, Mercedes. There will be plenty of time for answers on another day. Right now, you just need to lie back and rest. If you don't rest, your recovery period will be much longer. I can tell you as far as your memory goes, you should regain most of your memory. If anything, when you're talking, you may feel a little weird. This is due to the injury your brain has suffered. Anytime a person suffers a traumatic brain injury, we can only speculate as to the amount of damage the brain has received. So far, the swelling of your brain has been your biggest issue."

Mercedes listened as best she could. She was so tired. Finally, not being able to stay awake, she fell asleep.

Drs. Lajonque and Satchai walked out the door into the hallway where Harper Pedosta and another woman they did not know were waiting for them.

Harper stopped Dr. Lajonque. "Well, Gerald, what's the story? Is Mercedes going to be all right?"

Dr. Satchai nodded to both women and told Dr. Lajonque she would see him when she made her evening rounds, and she walked down the hall to the doctors' lounge.

Dr. Lajonque shared what information he knew. The woman with Harper Pedosta listened intently. Finally, unable to keep quiet, she said, "Dr. Lajonque, my name is Harper

Angelique Pedosta. I am a distant relative of Harper Pedosta. I came here looking for something that belongs to our family. I found a diary belonging to my grandmother, and in it was information about the items I'm looking for."

Dr. Lajonque looked at this young woman. She appeared to be about the same age as Mercedes and held a slight resemblance to Harper Pedosta. He immediately thought to himself, *If this young woman thought she would get any information from Mercedes, she would be thinking the wrong way.* It would take time to see if this person was on the level or if she had just been following the happenings in Pedeaux and decided she would cash in on the adventure.

"It's a pleasure to meet you, Ms. Pedosta. Please excuse me, my first obligation is to one of my own patients who will be coming out of anesthesia soon. I'm afraid he won't really be too happy to see me after he wakes up from his surgery. Seems he will be barking an octave higher." Turning to leave with a laugh, Dr. Lajonque said, "I'll be back in a little while. I'll talk with you later, Harper."

As Dr. Lajonque walked out of the hospital, he noticed a red Bentley parked near the emergency room. Looking at the licensed tag, he read, "MYPLCNT." Thinking the license tag was strange, he also noticed the tag was from Maine. Maine was a long way from Ohio. Kind of a coincidence her showing up the same time as all this was happening to

THE House ON THE CORNER

Mercedes. *Think I'll stop by the sheriff's office to give him this latest development.*

Walking into the Sheriff's Office, Dr. Lajonque saw a group of deputies gathered around a desk. When they saw him, they immediately moved away from the desk. Curious, Dr. Lajonque walked over to the desk. Lying on top of the desk was a picture of the young Harper Pedosta who had just conveniently appeared on the scene after Mercedes had been attacked and ended up in the hospital. The particular image Harper Angelique Pedosta presented to the world was not the kind a mother and father would want on their mantle in their living room. Harper Angelique Pedosta (as she called herself) was dressed in a cropped football jersey with a very skimpy bikini bottom to cover the rest of her. She was standing in a very seductive pose. This being bent at the waist with her bottom facing the camera and her looking over her shoulder at the cameraman.

"Well, I certainly see why you all were standing here with your tongues hitting the floor. Just so you know, this young lady claims to be related to the Pedostas around here, so if I were you, I'd tread lightly," he said sternly.

Sheriff Winegard walked out of his office. "Come on in, Gerald. I have something to show you."

Dr. Lajonque walked into the sheriff's office. On the bulletin board were pictures of Al Pedosta, Aaron Pedosta, and the young man who hadn't been identified.

Sheriff Winegard opened his desk drawer and pulled out an envelope marked "Evidence" and said, "In this envelope is a map of Mercedes's house. This map shows there is something hidden in there and it belonged at one time to the Pedosta family. Mercedes has no business going back there until we can get this cleared up. I don't want to get a call that something has happened to her again. It is my suggestion that once she is able to leave the hospital, you take her back to the farm until this is all cleared up."

"Where did you get this map? Is the person who gave it to you the same person who is trying to kill off anyone interested in Mercedes's house?"

"I can only tell you the person who gave this to me is very close to Mercedes. She doesn't even know about this map. It was brought to me just after Mercedes was taken to the hospital. The person who gave it to me has a home scanner. They caught the call to Mercedes's house through the life squad. I had to promise not to divulge the name of the owner."

"What makes you believe the owner of the map is not the same person who hurt Mercedes? How do you know they didn't try to knock her in the head to gain access to her house?"

THE *House* ON THE CORNER

Sheriff Winegard just looked at Dr. Lajonque. "I'm telling you, for your own good, Gerald, I promised the person I would not give out their name. Just trust me, this person would never hurt Mercedes. They are tired of the killing. They want to set the record straight, but first we have to make sure we can find the killer or killers of these young men."

"Why in the world would this person want to wait, and what 'record' do they want to set straight? Did this person hire someone to get rid of Aaron and his brother? If anyone should be tired of this, it is Mercedes! She bought that house on the corner to write. It was going to be her safe place in the city where she could sit in her living room or den and look out the windows at the people walking and driving down the street. Mercedes is a visual person. She gets her best ideas from watching people. How in the hell do you stand there and tell me the person who had a map to Mercedes's house suddenly decides they are 'tired of the killing' but wants to remain anonymous? Please, don't even think I'll just smile and walk out the door and pretend I didn't hear this! Nope, I'm angry that someone's tried and almost succeeded in killing Mercedes. Do what you want, but I won't rest until I know Mercedes is safe and you have the person or persons who did this to her behind bars! Call me when you want to be honest and tell me what's really going on, Sheriff!" With this, Dr. Lajonque stalked out the door.

The Hospital

∾

Mercedes felt a hand on her head. The hand felt like her mother's did when she was feeling for a fever. Her eyelids felt heavy. She tried to open them, but it seemed to be taking a very long time for them to move. Finally, she opened her eyes. Trying to raise her head was another task. Looking out the corner of her right eye, she could see a window. It looked like it was early morning. She could see a ray of sunlight shining through the clouds like it does when the sun is just starting to come up. Hearing a noise, she tried to turn head to the left to see who was coming toward her. Unable to turn her head, she closed her eyes and drifted back to sleep.

∾

Sheriff Winegard got a cup of coffee. It was already a long night and now it was going to be a longer day. He knew he had seen the girl with Harper Pedosta. He decided to go through the Ohio Prison Files. Typing in the words "Marionville Women's Prison" and the years 2000 to 2012, the pictures started coming on the screen. After looking at the faces of dozens of women who had committed a felony, he found the one he was looking for. There, looking back at him was a picture of a very, very young "Harper Angelique

THE *House* ON THE CORNER

Pedosta." Funny, her name wasn't Harper, nor was her middle name Angelique, and her last name certainly wasn't Pedosta! Below the picture from the Marionville Women's Prison, it showed her name was Sara Elyn Nite. Typing her name on the Interstate Identification Index, Sheriff Winegard learned more about Sara Nite than he'd ever wanted to know.

Her rap sheet told a story of a young girl from Dayton, Texas, who was arrested as a prostitute at the age of ten. As a first offender, she'd received probation provided she would go to counseling and was released to the custody of her mother and father. From there, she would be arrested for destruction, damage, and vandalism of property at the age of fourteen. Sara had broken into the home of a junior high guidance counselor, slashed her brand-new sofa and loveseat, then stole the pictures of the guidance counselor's mother and father. These pictures would become Sara's. She would tell her friends they were her grandparents. (Sara's real grandparents died under mysterious circumstances while on vacation in Switzerland. The Swiss police were never able to find the murderer or the weapon that was used. It remains a cold case.) Again, she received probation with the stipulation that she and her parents seek family counseling.

A new picture of Sara appeared. At the age of nineteen, she was booked for extortion and blackmail. It was at this time that Sara's appearance would change. Going from a dark-haired, petite girl, she was now a blonde, about five feet four inches tall with blue eyes and braces on her teeth.

Sheriff Winegard scrolled on through the files on Sara. She had spent most of her teenage years and her young adult life in the prison system. Now it was time to find out exactly why she had taken on the persona of Harper Angelique Pedosta. Closing the computer, he wondered what involvement she may have had in the assault on Mercedes Adler.

Sheriff Winegard told the deputy on the desk he was going to the hospital. He figured Dr. Lajonque would have had enough time to go back to his vet's practice, take care of his patients, and get back to the hospital by this time.

Walking into Mercedes's room, Dr. Lajonque saw a note had been left on the stand by her bed. Picking it up, he read, "If you think I am through, you're wrong! What you have belongs to me, not you! Not now, not ever . . . you will be so sorry you have it. This was just a small taste of what I can do. I'll be waiting for you!"

Sue Coffey was the nurse assigned to Mercedes. The sheriff and the doctor agreed it would be in Mercedes's best interest to have someone stay in the room with her until she

THE *House* ON THE CORNER

was able to go home, then these same nurses would stay with her at her home.

Sue was a good nurse and a good person. She also was an experienced martial arts instructor, having received her black belt in karate the year before. This, in addition to Sue being an auxiliary sheriff's deputy holding the rank of lieutenant, made the return home somewhat safer for Mercedes.

The other two nurses, Toni Short and Jack Justice ("J. J.") were students at Mount Gillette Nursing School in a small town called Onesty, about twenty minutes from Pedeaux. Both young ladies were seniors looking forward to graduation the coming spring. Toni had a job waiting for her at Bloomburg Children's Hospital in Columbus, Ohio, and J. J. had a job waiting for her at Peaceful Acres nursing home in Pedeaux. Both would become the youngest directors of nursing in Ohio's history.

CHAPTER 14

Nursing Care

Dr. Lajonque asked Sue if she had seen anyone in the room. She said no but did remember seeing someone in the hall who had acted quite funny as she was coming down the hall to Mercedes's room. It was a young person who had a blue and silver hoodie on. She couldn't tell if it was a boy or girl, but whoever it was, they were walking fast.

Asking Sue for a pair of surgical gloves and something to put the note in, Dr. Lajonque proceeded to "bag the note" as evidence in the case.

As Sue was leaving, Sheriff Winegard walked into the room. Ignoring Dr. Lajonque, he walked directly to Mercedes's bedside and looked at the helpless woman lying on the bed. Taking her hand in his massive hands, he noticed something he hadn't seen when they were in Mercedes's room the last time. The numbers 1 to 10 were written on the back of her hand. He stood there thinking, wondering why someone would write those numbers on her hand. It meant something to the person who wrote it, but what would it mean to someone like Mercedes? When she got back to herself, he would ask her.

Dr. Lajonque placed Mercedes's hand back the way he'd found it and walked over to the chair to sit down and wait for any changes that might occur. While waiting, he started to doze off. Then he was wide awake again. He got out of the chair, walked over to the bedside table, pulled it open, and found a piece of paper. Pulling the food tray over to himself, he lowered it and began writing on the paper. He started from the first time Mercedes told him about Aaron Pedosta. Then he wrote down everything he could recall about the two boys at the college, and again he noted down his memories of the two girls in front of his vet's office. *Could one of them have been the girl calling herself Harper Angelique Pedosta?* he wondered. Then he thought about the meeting with Harper Pedosta at her farm. *What part did she really play in all this, and what was her connection regarding the house on the corner?* Did someone leave something in there and all these people know what it is or possibly know it is hidden in Mercedes's house and now they want to get in there and retrieve it? *Questions, questions, always another question!*

As Dr. Lajonque sat studying what he had written, Sheriff Winegard walked into Mercedes's room. "Sorry about that, Gerald," he said as he sat in the chair next to Dr. Lajonque. "How's our girl doing? Any changes?"

"No, the medicine she's taking is keeping her sedated. I'm not sure what the dosage is, but I would say it might be too much. Think I'll stop by the desk on my way out to see what they are giving her. She may be having a reaction to it," Dr. Lajonque spoke frankly.

Dr. Lajonque walked over by Mercedes's bed. As he stood staring at her, he noticed something he hadn't seen when he was there earlier. Mercedes always wore four rings. One looked like a large diamond. It was in a square setting, and the stone was actually a prism. When the light or sun would hit it, it would sparkle. She wore this ring on her left hand on her ring finger. Also on the left hand, she wore a silver ring in the shape of an exercise saddle with a thin, gold strap around it. This ring she wore on her index finger. Even though it really wasn't a saddle, she would get many compliments about it. On her right hand, she would change the ring on her ring finger to one that would match whatever top she would be wearing. On the index finger, she wore a solid silver ring with a horse head engraved on it. The horse head looked just like her Appaloosa "Chief" she'd had to put down a few years earlier because of chronic foundering in his hooves. This would be her favorite ring. When she realized he would never get any better, that he would have more bad days than good and his quality of life was being compromised by the constant pain, Mercedes put the welfare of her horse before her own desires. One frosty fall day, Dr. Lajonque met Mercedes with Chief in the field next to Mercedes's farm house with one syringe filled with sodium thiocyanate, a quick acting drug that would cause Chief's heart to stop instantly. Chief went down in less than thirty seconds. Mercedes had called Kevin Rains, a farmer down the road, the night before and explained what she was doing. She asked him to bring his backhoe down to dig a hole deep enough to bury the sixteen-hand Appaloosa.

The hole Kevin dug was about eight and a half feet deep. When Kevin had the hole finished, he assisted Mercedes and Dr. Lajonque in burying Chief. Mercedes could look out her dining room every evening and see where her beloved horse was buried. She knew he'd loved that field where the grass was always so lush and green in the spring.

It was odd; the one thing this horse loved the most would actually be the reason he would die. Dr. Lajonque made a mental note to call Dr. Straw, Mercedes's family doctor. Being there was no other relative to discuss her health with, Mercedes's doctor had no problems talking about her health with Dr. Lajonque.

Nursing Care

Sheriff Winegard's cell phone went off. Taking it out of his vest, he saw the call was a text message from his deputy, Matt Penne. The message read, "Just got a call from someone who said they overheard one of the nurses talking in the hall at the hospital about Mercedes, something about tonight being the night. Didn't know if someone was going to do something at the hospital or to her house here in town or to her farm. Just know something's up as the person who heard it only heard what I just wrote down."

Sheriff Winegard pulled his radio mic off his shoulder. Putting it to his mouth, then pressing the button he said, "I need two deputies to go to Mercedes Adler's farm on Huntington Road. Get there as fast as possible. Do not use sirens. I repeat, do not use sirens. Call me when you get there, I've got further instructions." Turning to Dr. Lajonque, he told him what was happening.

"I'm going out to Mercedes's house. You can either come with me or drive yourself."

Sheriff Winegard and Dr. Lajonque hustled out of Mercedes's room. Looking at Dr. Lajonque, the sheriff said, "I'm sending a deputy to Mercedes's house on the corner. I'm instructing him to call Brian Sams, the chief of police, to have some of his men meet him there as well. We're also bringing in the state patrol, and I'm posting someone here to watch over Mercedes and the people here in the hospital."

THE *House* ON THE CORNER

As they left the hospital, walking to the sheriff's cruiser, Dr. Lajonque said, "Okay, Bill, now's not the time to keep things close to your chest. I want to know what is going on."

Sheriff Winegard then told Dr. Lajonque about the phone call. "We're going to Mercedes's farm. If anything, this person or these people, whichever, will think we're going to her house on the corner. I've learned over the years, if you try to think like them, then sometimes you're able to figure their next move. I don't know how many people are involved in this. I do know for sure there is no 'Harper Angelique Pedosta.' The person who is pretending to be her is really a convicted felon named Sara Nite. She was just released from the Marionville Women's Prison after serving seven years for a series of crimes. It looks like the older this young woman has gotten, the more violent her crimes have become. I haven't figured out how she became involved with Harper Pedosta yet."

Dr. Lajonque stared out the window as the cruiser moved effortlessly down the county road. They would have to go through a small village that had at one time had shown the promise of becoming a "town," but with the Depression, growth stopped, and now only a few hundred people lived in the village. As they drove through, Sheriff Winegard watched for anything that seemed out of place. Since all this business with Mercedes and the Pedosta family, he had become more aware of how people reacted or looked.

Stopping at a four-way stop, Dr. Lajonque looked over to his right. There, standing in the door of a deserted building, stood the young man he had seen at the hospital. The young man saw Dr. Lajonque as well, and when he did, he immediately leaned back into the darkness where he could no longer be seen.

"Stop the car, stop the car!" Dr. Lajonque demanded. As Sheriff Winegard pulled the cruiser around the corner, Dr. Lajonque jumped out. While he was running to the back of the building, Sheriff Winegard ran to the front. Busting out the back door, the young man tried to knock Dr. Lajonque down; however, Dr. Lajonque did not move, and he brought his arm up and hit the young man in his throat. The young man fell down onto his back. Grabbing his throat and coughing, the young man tried to get up as Dr. Lajonque pushed him back down. In the meantime, Sheriff Winegard came running around the building, gun drawn.

"Well, Gerald, what have we here? Appears you have stopped this fella. How do you know him?" Sheriff Winegard asked.

"He was at the hospital the day they brought Mercedes in. He stayed there until the doctor came out and told us Mercedes was going to be all right, after which he left when

THE *House* ON THE CORNER

I looked at him. He really didn't do anything wrong, just sat there, and when he saw me watching him, he got up, went to the vending machine, got a candy bar, and sat back down. As I said before, once the doctor came out, he left. I thought his behavior was odd, then I saw him lurking in the doorway. We're not too far away from Mercedes's farm, wouldn't you say? Think we should ask him some questions?" exclaimed Dr. Lajonque.

CHAPTER 15

Road Trip

Sheriff Winegard helped Dr. Lajonque lift the young man to his feet. "What's your name? Do you live around here?" he asked. The young man frowned and tried to pull away from the two men. When he saw it was going to be a fruitless effort, he finally opened his mouth and said, "My name is Paul Revere. I ride a horse every night through the village. I keep watch for the British. If I see any, I let the people know so they can hide. The British will steal their children and sell them for slaves."

Sheriff Winegard looked at the young man like he could not believe his ears. Showing his major agitation at him he said, "Look, I don't know who you are, I much less care if you think you're Paul Revere or Superman. There will be a couple of deputies here in a few minutes to take you to the Compton County sheriff's office. Since you don't want to tell me who

THE *House* ON THE CORNER

you are, I'll run your prints. At this time, you will be charged with obstruction of justice and trespassing." With this, Sheriff Winegard read the young man his Miranda rights. He then pulled the phone from his shoulder and called the two deputies to come to pick the young man up.

As the deputies were driving away, Dr. Lajonque and Sheriff Winegard went into the empty building the young man was seen in. In it they found two sleeping bags, a machete, a .38 caliber pistol with four boxes of bullets, a .410 shotgun and shells, and finally, various types of knives. All of these things were in a four-foot metal box with silk lining. Someone had gone to a lot of trouble to put that lining in the box. It looked almost like a coffin for a small child more than a gun case.

Also in the room were dirty clothes, shoes, and underwear belonging to a woman. There was no sign of identification, billfolds, purses, or anything that would tell the sheriff who these people were. Dr. Lajonque looked around at the room. Then he decided to go out and look at the rest of the building. Walking around the corner into what would have been the kitchen, he saw something that made him call the sheriff into the kitchen. As Sheriff Winegard walked into the kitchen, he saw what Dr. Lajonque was looking at. There, on the countertop, were pictures of Mercedes Adler, Dr.

Lajonque, and Harper Pedosta. There was also a picture of Mercedes's house on the corner and directions to her farm.

After looking at these, Sheriff Winegard called his office and requested the forensics team respond to the building in the village. He then requested two more cruisers with deputies to follow him to Mercedes's farm. He also called the Ohio State Highway Patrol and requested their assistance at the farm.

The drive to the farm took less than five minutes. Pulling in the long driveway, they made their plans of where to start. First, though, they would wait for their backup. It didn't take long for the sheriff's deputies and the Ohio State Highway Patrol to line up behind the sheriff's cruiser.

CHAPTER 16

Road Trip

Getting out of the cruiser, Dr. Lajonque and Sheriff Winegard walked over to the men and women waiting for further instruction. Sheriff Winegard sent a detail to the barn and the two smaller buildings near the barn. Another detail went to the run-in shed across from the grain bin, while one went to the grain bin. The rest entered Mercedes's house after being told not to disturb anything, but if they found anything, they were to wait for further orders.

Entering Mercedes's house, two deputies went to the basement, two highway patrolmen went upstairs, and Dr. Lajonque and the sheriff went to clear the rooms on the first floor. Dr. Lajonque went into the library and found the books were strewn over the floor and the drawers in the desk were pulled out, as were the drawers in the filing cabinets in the dining room. In the two back rooms, one of which was used as a utility room, the washer and dryer were pulled away from the wall. The rack that held clothes was on the floor. Wash soap as well as other cleaning supplies were thrown around the room. The closet door was open, and coats and jackets were pulled from their hangers. In the room where Mercedes spent most of her time (the one she called the "summer kitchen"), she had bookshelves as well. Books were pulled from these shelves like the ones in the library.

Sheriff Winegard asked the captain of the highway patrol to call the Bureau of Criminal Investigation in London, Ohio, to come to the farm. The forensics team called to tell the sheriff they had finished their investigation of the old building where they found the young man and they had their findings ready. Asking if there was anything that would give them an idea of why he had Mercedes and Dr. Lajonque's pictures, they said yes. He told them to send their report back to the sheriff's office with a deputy and to come out to the farm. He had more work for them there, and he wanted them to work with the people from the bureau.

~

Mercedes woke up. This time she wasn't feeling as sleepy as she had earlier. She felt around on the bed, found the control, and pushed the button to raise her head. She sat up for

THE House ON THE CORNER

the first time. How long she had been there she wasn't sure, but she knew she had been there a while, as the little piece of hair on her chin had grown out. Anytime she took a shower, she always "shaved" there to keep it from growing. She'd had an elderly aunt who had a bit of a beard. Mercedes didn't want to be like her.

Sitting in a chair across from Mercedes's bed was a Compton County sheriff's deputy. Her name was Molly Bollafare. She had been with the dheriff's department for twenty-five years. This was the first time she was asked to sit with someone. She would have rather been out to Ms. Adler's farm helping, but the way Sheriff Winegard had explained it, it was more important for her to be with Ms. Adler as she appeared to be in some kind of danger, and he knew Molly would be of greater service there.

A young woman walked into Mercedes's room. Surprised by seeing the deputy sitting in the chair, she said she was in the wrong room and left. Watching her leave, Deputy Molly got out of her chair and walked to the door, watching for the young woman. She spotted her across from the nurses' station. Taking out her cell phone, she called Sheriff Winegard and reported the incident. He told her to stay with Mercedes and he would get back to her.

Deputy Molly watched as the young woman got on the elevator. It headed down. Molly watched as the elevator went all the way to the lobby. Molly knew when the elevator door opened, there would be two deputies waiting for the young woman. They would take her to the station to question her regarding entering a hospital room that was restricted to people who had been cleared by Dr. Lajonque and the sheriff. Besides, she was just a little bit *too* surprised to see Molly there.

Mercedes watched as Molly contacted Sheriff Winegard. Not being able to hear what Molly said to him, Mercedes watched her watching the young woman. Finally, Molly turned, and seeing Mercedes watching her, she walked over to her bed. Standing there, she explained she was there for Mercedes's safety.

Mercedes didn't understand what Molly was saying. She kept wondering, *Why does this woman need to be here?* Mercedes finally figured out she was in the hospital and she must have been in some kind of accident. What she couldn't figure out was why this deputy would stay in her room. Finally, she moved her head back down with her remote and went back to sleep.

She thought if she went back to sleep, the next time she woke up, Dr. Lajonque might be there, and he'd explain what was going on. *This is all so confusing.*

THE *House* ON THE CORNER

Dr. Lajonque couldn't believe the mess. As he was looking in the summer kitchen, he noticed something in the corner of the room. Walking over to it, he saw it was a piece of paper with writing on it. Picking it up with just his index finger and thumb, he walked over to the window where the sun was shining through. Holding the paper up, he saw it was the same writing as the note in Mercedes's hospital room. The paper said, "I was here and you were gone; now you're here and I'm gone. I know you; you don't know me. Give me what belongs to me and you won't ever have to see me again! If you don't, you won't be able to see anyone as you'll be in a place where it won't make a difference!" The note wasn't signed.

Looking around, Dr. Lajonque opened the cupboard and found a box of sandwich bags. Pulling one out, he placed the note inside the bag. Walking back in the library, he found Sheriff Winegard looking at something. "What is it, Sheriff? You look like you saw a ghost."

Sheriff Winegard turned and looked at Dr. Lajonque and said, "Look at this, Gerald. I pulled it out from under the leather wingback chair. These people are crazy. I wouldn't doubt it if Mercedes had come back here for something and one of these people were here, they would have killed her. God knows they tried to kill her at her house in town, but I figure they must have gotten scared off."

Dr. Lajonque looked at the picture in the sheriff's hand. It was another picture of Mercedes. She was standing beside her horse Chief. She had a smile on her face. Someone had drawn a noose around her neck, made blood come out of her eyes and mouth, then written the words, "Can't wait till I make her look like this!"

Shaking his head, Dr. Lajonque placed the picture into the sandwich bag with the note. No one said anything. They were all standing around, thinking their own thoughts.

Dr. Lajonque wondered why it was so hard to find whoever was responsible for doing these things. He felt like he was trespassing on Mercedes's private belongings, but he knew if she were here, she would, of course, urge him to look around.

Walking up the stairs, he stopped at the first landing, and looking out the window, he saw the garage. As he stood there looking at the garage, his peripheral vision caught sight of movement, someone running. Looking toward the road, he saw there were two figures running under the bridge. He turned, ran down the stairs, and yelled for Sheriff Winegard and the deputies to follow him.

Running out the door, Dr. Lajonque spotted a running cruiser and jumped into the driver's seat. By the time he put it in gear, Sheriff Winegard was in the passenger seat beside him. Other deputies had gotten to their cars and were right behind him.

Speeding down the driveway, Dr. Lajonque turned right and drove up the hill. He then turned into another drive beside a barn. Jumping out, he ran to the gate, opened it, and took off running as fast as he could chasing the two figures who were running for their lives across the field.

Sheriff Winegard ordered the deputies to go down the road to the first road to their right. This way if the two fugitives were to get away from Dr. Lajonque, then they would have to come out on that road where his deputies would be there waiting for them.

Looking behind the barn, Sheriff Winegard saw two figures approaching the barn on horseback. They were riding at a canter. When they got to the barn, Sheriff Winegard saw the two riders were Mercedes's neighbors from the farm down the road, Derby and Dell Sallon. These two young ladies were visiting their grandmother, Ms. Derby A. Sallon. Seeing all the lights and activity, they were curious about what was going on; but the Sheriff instructed them not to go to the field where Dr. Lajonque was chasing the two figures. He explained they could be carrying weapons and might be dangerous. Just to be safe, the girls were to either stay at the barn, or turn and go back to their own farm. They decided to stay.

Road Trip

In the meantime, Dr. Lajonque was becoming winded. *Damn cigarettes!* he thought as he kept chasing the two figures. Whoever these two were, they didn't seem the least bit winded. Just as he was about to slow down, one of the figures tripped over a corn stalk and landed face-first on the ground. The other one kept running.

Dr. Lajonque came up on the figure on the ground and turned the stunned runner over. Pulling the ski mask off, he was surprised to see the face of Harper Angelique Pedosta. She was dressed in black again. This time, though, her hair wasn't dark like it was at the hospital; it was blonde. As she sputtered, trying to get the dirt from her mouth and her nostrils, she began fighting, trying to get up. When she finally gave up and opened her eyes, she was shocked to see Dr. Lajonque sitting on her. "Get off me, fat ass!" Dr. Lajonque just sat there. He wouldn't have moved if there'd been an earthquake. There was no way he would get up and let this piece of trash get away. He really didn't know how much she was involved; he did know though she had been in Mercedes's house and was looking for something. He decided to catch his breath and wait on the sheriff. Then, and only then, would he get off her.

The other figure stopped long enough to see Harper Angelique Pedosta on the ground with some big man on top of her. *Too bad*, she thought. She knew if she could get to

THE *House* ON THE CORNER

the main road, she could flag down a vehicle and get away. Little did she know, the whole road was covered not just with county deputies, but the state highway patrol as well. There would be no way she would get away.

Running was easy for this person. She was an all-state distance runner when she was in high school and had even made the junior Olympic team. She could have gone on had she not gotten involved with steroids. After a long run, she would develop excruciating leg cramps. The doctors prescribed steroids on which she became dependent. After the last meet she'd run, she was tested for drugs, and her life took a downhill turn. She was removed from the junior Olympic team. Once the college officials found out about the drug problem, they wanted nothing to do with her, and her scholarship offers were withdrawn.

It was at this time she became involved with J. K. Kabel, whose real name was John Kash Kabel. He was wonderful. He had contacts with all kinds of people who could get her all the steroids she wanted or needed. As long as she had cash, J. K. would keep her supplied. If for some reason she didn't have the cash, he would "farm her out" to pimps and friends to get the money for her addiction. He had done this for another girl who he'd kept on the string for years, the unfortunate Sara Nite.

Road Trip

J. K. remembered a young man named Al Pedosta who bragged he had a rich relative who had left money and jewels somewhere in Pedeaux. Thinking Al was just full of smoke, J. K. didn't think anything about the missing treasure until he heard Al had been killed. Al's murder appeared to be a mystery until his brother Aaron was killed. No one had been arrested, and the killings remained unsolved. Always a man with an eye for opportunity, J. K. thought this sad turn of events may be a blessing in disguise. If there were a fortune hidden somewhere, then he would be the one who would find it. After all, no one really knew if the stories were true. There was one way to find out, and he would use every way and everyone he knew to find it.

The girl stopped when she got to the road. Taking deep breaths, she felt the pain in the shins of her legs. Sometimes if she stretched, the pain would go away. Finally, the pain started to subside. Looking down the road, she saw headlights approaching. Sprinting to the other side of the road, she started to hitchhike. Watching the car get closer, it dawned on her it wasn't just any car, it was a sheriff's cruiser! Turning on her heel, she took off for the field. The deputy saw the girl at the edge of his lights. Knowing this was one of the ones Dr. Lajonque was chasing, he slammed the car into park, pushed the radio phone, and called into the sheriff's' office. He told them he was pursuing a suspect on foot across the

THE *House* ON THE CORNER

Myers' field. He asked for backup as he knew if she got to the woods, he would lose her.

Sheriff Winegard heard the call. As he ran to his cruiser, he called for Dr. Lajonque, who had just assisted a deputy in putting Sara Nite into the back of the cruiser. Running to the car, Dr. Lajonque opened the door and jumped in.

Sheriff Winegard was excited. Maybe now they could finally get the whole story and find out how these two young women were involved in the ransacking of Mercedes's homes and possibly the murders of the Pedosta boys.

Driving down the road, the two men appeared lost in their own thoughts. Dr. Lajonque was trying to figure out the two young women. Horrified, he thought to himself, *They had to be delusional, psychotic, or worse yet, completely void of conscience.* He pulled his cell phone from his inside jacket pocket and called the hospital to check on Mercedes. The hospital phone kept ringing. Finally, an operator answered. Dr. Lajonque explained to the operator who he was. He then asked to be connected to Dr. Sharp's cell phone.

Dr. Sharp's voice came on stating he was not available to take the call. Dr. Lajonque left a message for him to return his call, telling him he was just wondering how Mercedes was doing.

Sheriff Winegard was also thinking about the events that led up to where they were now. Then, the radio came alive: "Shots fired, shots fired!" came the voice over the radio. "Officer down, get the squad out here quick. He's bleeding real bad! I'm out here near the Myers' woods off Pasue Road. They'll need to come in off State Route 52, there's no other way to get back here. Hurry, damn it, hurry up!"

Sheriff Winegard turned on the emergency lights and pushed the accelerator down. As he maneuvered through the curves, Dr. Lajonque held on. Turning onto Pasue Road, he saw the sheriff's cruiser in the ditch. "Gerald, get out, look in the cruiser, see if Sara Nite is in there." Doing as Sheriff Winegard asked, Dr. Lajonque got out of the cruiser and walked over the to one in the ditch. In the back seat was Sara Nite. Her eyes were open, and she was staring straight ahead. On the side of her head was a hole about the size of a dime. Blood was trickling from the hole down onto the girl's collar, which was fast becoming a bright red.

Dr. Lajonque thought about how much tragedy had happened since Mercedes had decided to move her writing operation to Pedeaux. He really wanted to know the whole story about the young women, one of whom he hadn't met nor had any idea even existed.

Sheriff Winegard walked to the cruiser. Seeing Sara Nite was indeed dead, he called for the county coroner to come out. About this time, the backup units arrived, and they started securing the crime scene. Sheriff Winegard looked around, wondering, *Where is the deputy who'd been driving this cruiser?* He should have been in or near the cruiser. Looking on the ground, he saw footprints walking away from the driver's door toward the road. Was the deputy okay? Was he hurt? Taking the mic from his shoulder, he called central office. "Have you heard anything from Doug?" The dispatcher reported she had not heard anything from him since the deputy had left Mercedes's farm with Sara Nite in the backseat of the cruiser.

Looking at Dr. Lajonque, Sheriff Winegard told him no call had been made to the office about the crime scene. No deputy asking for assistance or a life squad or anything else. The dispatcher told him she had wondered why it was taking him so long to get back to the office with Sara Nite.

Just as Dr. Lajonque started to say something, he saw a flash of light reflected by the Sheriff's badge. As he turned to see where it was coming from, he heard something "zing" by his ear. Looking out into the distance, he saw a darkly clad figure running toward the woods. Everything seemed to shift into slow motion. The sheriff was holding his shoulder, and blood was dripping through his fingers. He was staring at the blood like he couldn't figure out where it came from. The EMTs were yelling at the other deputies, telling them the sheriff had been hit.

The county coroner was running, but it didn't appear to Dr. Lajonque he was in any hurry. It was like his feet were

Road Trip

really heavy, and they couldn't move any quicker. Finally, it all became too real. Everyone was running around, looking for where the shot came from. As Dr. Lajonque eased the wounded man to the ground, he told him he had seen the dark clad figure run into the woods.

Borrowing the sheriff's mic, Dr. Lajonque called the dispatcher. Trying to talk with her as the coroner was pushing gauze packs into the Sheriff's shoulder, he instructed her to call in auxiliary deputies along with the mounted patrol and get them out to the Pasue Road location as soon as possible.

The coroner ordered Sara Nite's body taken out of the cruiser. The crime scene unit dusted the car for fingerprints and took pictures of Sara Nite before the body was removed and they looked at the footprints near the door.

Deputy Ben Acker, a twenty-five year veteran of the force, pointed out the fact that only one set of footprints led away from the cruiser. This had to be the deputy's footprints. As they were discussing this, one of the auxiliary deputies walked up with his dog. Raring to go, he asked, "Baron and I are ready to go; is this where we start?"

Dr. Lajonque nodded in the affirmative, and the dog and deputy were off and running. The dog was making a yelping noise, causing birds, fox, deer, rabbits, and any other four-legged creature to scurry off to the nearest hiding place. The tracks led to a small, though well-constructed, barn in a clearing. Calling from his portable radio, the deputy told Sheriff Winegard about the find.

Sheriff Winegard instructed the deputy to stay where he was and keep the dog as quiet as he could. The sheriff didn't want to alert anyone who might still be around, especially if they were hiding in the barn. In short order, Sheriff Winegard, Dr. Lajonque, and a group of deputies had surrounded the barn.

Taking a bullhorn from one of the four-wheelers, Sheriff Winegard announced the barn was surrounded by the police and instructed anyone in the barn to "come out with their hands in the air."

Waiting for what seemed like an eternity, Dr. Lajonque heard the *click* of a gun behind him. Turning slowly, he met face to face with Deputy Pete Buttons. "Don't move, Doc!" Deputy Buttons said. "It's been rough these past few years, what with the recession and all. I couldn't take a chance on Sara spilling her guts and me losing everything I've worked for all these years. She wasn't anyone special, had no parents around close, don't really know if they're even alive.

"Picked her up at the truck stop. She was out there hooking for a ride out west. We had gotten a call saying there were 'lot lizards' out there bugging the truckers. It was then it dawned on me I could use her. So I told her if she helped me out, I wouldn't turn her in. I would even get her a plane ticket to wherever she wanted to go. Then I heard you all talking about Mercedes Adler and what all was going on with her and it dawned on me if there was indeed a fortune laying around somewhere close, why should she have it?!"

Dr. Lajonque continued to stare at the deputy. He was trying very hard not to turn his eyes to the barrel of the gun that was coming up to Pete Buttons's head.

"If you even have the nerve to breathe wrong, I'll blow your brains from here to kingdom come! Now, put down your gun, raise your hands, and back away from Dr. Lajonque. Do it, now!" said Sheriff Winegard.

Deputy Pete Buttons dropped the gun and did as he was told. Taking his handcuffs off his belt, Sheriff Winegard tossed them to another deputy and told him to put them on Deputy Buttons and take him with one of the other deputies to the county jail with the instructions that no one, not even the media, was to talk to Buttons. He was to be held in solitary confinement until the sheriff returned to file formal charges.

Sheriff Winegard looked at Dr. Lajonque and asked if he was all right. Dr. Lajonque nodded yes. The sheriff shook his head. "Just when you think you know someone, they do something like this. I heard everything he said to you, but I don't believe he was the ringleader in this. Not that he wasn't smart enough, I just don't see him with the ability to plan it out. Whoever the other woman is who was in this with Sara Nite is the planner. I come near saying she was the one who talked Pete into turning the blind eye for Sara, promising him a cut from the fortune plus whatever else Sara was ordered to do for Pete."

Dr. Lajonque looked at the Sheriff. "How about having someone take me to my car? I need to get to the hospital with Mercedes. It's hard to tell how many people are involved in this. If the other young woman is still around, she could be setting up a plan to hurt Mercedes." The Sheriff nodded in agreement. The deputy pulled up. Dr. Lajonque got in the cruiser and was taken back to his car at the hospital where he had left it when they went to Mercedes's farm.

He got out of the cruiser and walked around his car to make sure it was safe. Walking into the hospital, he was surprised to see Harper Pedosta standing in the lobby as if she'd been waiting for him. "Have you seen Mercedes this afternoon? I went to her room and she wasn't there," she asked in a worried voice.

Pulling out his cell phone, he called Mercedes's doctor, who told him he had not released her, nor had he ordered any tests. If anything, she was scheduled for a CAT scan the next day. She was then scheduled for physical therapy as her speech was somewhat affected by the blow she took to her head.

Dr. Lajonque explained to Harper Pedosta the events that had taken place that day. "Now, we have to find Mercedes," he said.

Going up to the floor where Mercedes's room was, Dr. Lajonque went into her room. Looking around for something that would tell him what had taken place, he saw on the floor a piece of the bandage that was holding Mercedes's IV. A pair of tweezers was lying on Mercedes's nightstand. Taking the tweezers, he picked up the piece of bandage and placed it in a plastic bag that was on the end of the bed.

Harper Pedosta was looking around as well. Seeing that none of Mercedes's clothes were missing, she had to assume Mercedes had been taken against her will. Not seeing anything that she thought she could do to help, she walked to the nurses' station. Helen Rider, night nurse, was watching as these two people looked very worried about the woman who had been in that room. *They should be worried*, she thought. Once Mercedes told her where she hid the fortune that was left by the previous owners, then she would make sure Dr. Lajonque and Harper Pedosta would never find the body of Ms. Mercedes Adler.

Helen Rider came to Pedeaux, Ohio, with a master's degree in nursing. She had been the lead trainer for nursing classes at the community college for several years. When automation started at the college, online classes were established.

THE *House* ON THE CORNER

It was no longer necessary to have one-on-one classes. Even nursing classes could be completed online. The only time she would even be remotely involved with her students was assigning students to clinicals at nearby hospitals or nursing homes. This is why she'd taken the job at the hospital. She thought she wasn't getting paid what she was really worth, but it was better than working in a nursing home.

Nurse Rider had not come to Pedeaux by chance. She had been born in a small town near Pedeaux called Owenton. Her parents had the only grocery store for twenty-five miles. They were hard workers; went to the Baptist church every Sunday, and felt the Lord had blessed them when their daughter Helen was born. They both were middle-aged by the time Helen came into the world. She'd started to care for her parents at a very young age. She graduated at the top of her class from high school and received an academic scholarship to Ashball College in Pedeaux, Ohio. She excelled there and graduated magna cum laude. She had also been inducted into the Beta Beta Beta Honor Society.

When Helen left college, she was offered the job as director of nursing for Pinecross Community College. Here she would establish a nursing program that would gain honors in the state for the fine group of licensed practical nurses and registered nurses that would graduate from this college. In Helen's view, the problems started when the college's board kept changing presidents. Each new one would have their own agenda. The programs that cost the most were the ones cut first. They never understood if a program were to be successful, it would cost money to keep up with the times to make it successful, so when Helen would go to the board with a new request for the latest technology or a new piece of equipment, the board would invariably turn it down.

The program started losing students. They found schools that were more modern, where they could train with the latest equipment. Helen would now be operating basically a barebones program. The board took the student enrollment for nursing classes from one hundred to fifty in less than two years. These fifty would not necessarily be the best and brightest, but they could pass a state nursing test and that would be it. The program started suffering, and the more Helen begged for more money to improve the course, the more firmly the board refused. That was it, and Helen joined the staff at the local hospital, always working the night shift as this shift would pay more than the others, plus no one else wanted it.

Harper Pedosta walked over to the nurses' station. "Nurse Rider, did you see anyone taking Mercedes from her room today?" Nurse Rider looked at her and said, "I just came on board a little while ago. There was nothing in report about

Ms. Adler having tests or anything. Isn't she in her room? I hadn't gotten a chance to go in and see her."

"I'm not trying to be smart or anything, it's just if she were in the room, why would I come out here and ask you if you've seen her," Harper Pedosta replied.

"Well, I say let's go look for her," Nurse Rider said. "I'll call the other floors and alert them she's missing also." *Little do you know, Mercedes is somewhere where no one will find her,* thought Nurse Rider. *You can look and look. Tear up the hospital, put out all points bulletins and call the FBI, CIA, or any other place you want to call, but that still won't find her.* She smiled to herself as she thought these thoughts.

In the meantime, Mercedes felt drugged. She had just eaten a little applesauce for lunch as her stomach was upset. Dr. Lajonque had left in a hurry with the sheriff. She thought it tasted a little odd, but as bad as she felt, she wasn't going to worry about it. Now, as she tried to wake up, she felt very, very cold. *Was it cold outside?* She knew it was fall, but it hadn't been getting cold. *Was she still in the hospital and in her room?* This didn't feel like her room. It felt cold and dark. Her room at the hospital was light and cheery.

Finally, getting her eyes opened, she saw she was in a room that was dark. There was no light, only a small window near the ceiling. *Was she in an attic? How did she get here? Where was Deputy Molly?* She heard someone scream, and she realized it was herself. She got quiet again. Then she heard the footsteps. They came close to the door. She thought whoever they belonged to would open the door, but they didn't. She heard them go down the stairs. She knew it had to be stairs by the way their feet hit when they were walking.

She found it difficult to figure out if she was indeed in an attic. She tried to move her feet, but they were tied together with something. Her hands were free. This made no sense. Didn't the person who'd tied her feet know she could get loose? Reaching down, she felt her ankles. No wonder they weren't worrying about her getting away. Her ankles were tied with plastic zip ties. She knew the only way to get them off was to cut them. She didn't know what time it was or how long she had been here. *Who is doing this to me?* she wondered. *Why are they doing this?*

At last, it dawned on her that Dr. Lajonque didn't know where she was. She wondered if anyone would be able to find her. The door opened. She couldn't see because the light behind whoever it was blinded her. She could smell the person. They smelled like old, moldy clothes. This person was above her; she could feel their breath. The next thing she knew they had grabbed her arm and she'd felt a sting, and then her arm burned. It wasn't long before she was asleep again.

The person looking down at Mercedes wondered when other people would be there to help him with Mercedes.

THE *House* ON THE CORNER

God, he hoped they would get there soon so they could get the treasure and get out of Pedeaux. They really hated this place! Why they'd brought Mercedes here was not clear to this person, only that they wanted to make sure no one would find her for a very, very long time.

◈

Dr. Lajonque was on the phone with his office. He had called in another veterinarian to take over the practice while he tried to find Mercedes. The sheriff had notified the press of the kidnapping, and Dr. Lajonque was offering a sizeable reward for any information that led to the arrest and conviction of the kidnapper or kidnappers.

◈

Helen Rider waited on the phone call. It came about midnight. They had Mercedes Adler and had taken her to the place Helen had instructed. The other man had left. The man on the phone didn't know where he'd gone. Helen felt a tinge of remorse after seeing Sara Nite had been killed, but she knew Sara would sing like a canary if they had gotten her to the sheriff's office. *Too bad about the deputy.* She'd thought he was stronger, only to find out he fit the profile for every other man she had been with in her life. Starting out, he'd been attentive, always saying things to make her laugh, bringing her little presents. But when he'd finally gotten what he wanted from her, he changed—became too busy to talk with her and always had an excuse for not seeing her.

When she came up with the plan to get the fortune she thought Mercedes knew about, she called him to ask advice. He wanted in on it and would help. Helen saw this as a way to always know where the sheriff and his deputies were at all times. She agreed to give him part of it knowing in the back of her mind he would never see a dime.

The deputy's name was Gene Lable. He had been with the Compton County sheriff's department for twenty-four years. Gene thought he had seen everything there was to see, but every once in a while, someone would do something, and he would be surprised again.

This time was different. He met Helen Rider on a routine traffic stop. He got her on a redlight violation in a little village just outside of Pedeaux. The village had only one traffic light, and Helen ran it. She tried to talk her way out of it, and it worked. Gene thought she was the prettiest woman he had seen in a long time. When he asked her to step out of the car, she laughed and opened the door. When she stepped out, he was surprised to see she was barely five foot tall, but her shoes would make her about five foot four. This was the beginning of a relationship that would climax in behavior that would cost Deputy Gene Lable his life.

When Helen's shift was over at the hospital, she drove to the place where Mercedes had been taken. She parked the car in the lot next to the building, got out of the car, and looked around to see if anyone was watching. She looked up at the windows of the building and, not seeing anything, she opened the door in the back of the building.

Not too many people knew about the door. A few years ago, an artist had blown into town and, being down on his luck, went to the city manager's office, showed him some photos of his work and offered to paint murals on the sides of various buildings around Pedeaux. It was on the side of one of these buildings a door was painted over to match the mural. Unless a person knew exactly where the door was, no one would have been able to see it.

When he'd finished the mural, the newcomer walked back to the door. Using a lockpick he just happened to keep in his pocket, he unlocked the door. Inside, he saw steps leading upstairs. He walked in, closed the door behind him, and went up the stairs. The stairway wasn't very wide. He thought it certainly wasn't made for someone overweight.

When he got to the top of the stairs, there was a small landing with another locked door. Walking across the landing, he again had to use his lockpick to open the door. The door was very old and had swelled over the years. Pushing as hard as he could, the door finally gave way.

When he stepped through the door, he found himself in a small room. He saw an old iron bed with a musty-looking mattress. There was an old dresser in the other corner. There was a small window high up on the far wall. He had to climb on an old chair that was sitting near the wall to reach it. Looking out the window, he saw he was in the attic of the oldest hotel in Pedeaux.

Climbing down, he walked over to the dresser and pulled the top drawer open. Inside were old newspaper clippings. Taking them out of the drawer, he walked over to where the light was shining through the window. Looking at the clippings, he saw they were dated twenty-five years before. One showed a picture of a dog in a creek near a bridge. The paper told the story of a dog that was found drowned in the creek, but the story didn't end there. It went on to report the discovery of the body of a teenage girl who was found on the other side of the same bridge caught in a watering gate.

No one would have ever seen the body if the brush that was covering it hadn't blown away from strong winds that came in the weekend the body was found.

The artist folded the papers, walked back to the dresser, and stuck the papers back in the drawer.

THE *House* ON THE CORNER

It would be here the artist would spend his nights. No one ever knew about his room in the attic of the old hotel. Most people who stayed in the hotel thought maybe the hotel was really haunted.

After becoming addicted to drugs, the artist eventually overdosed and died. His body was found in the alley behind the hotel. Being that no one knew where he came from or who his family was, he would be buried in a pauper's grave in the cemetery in Pedeaux.

Helen Rider found the door painted into the mural on the old hotel's wall one day when she'd visited the farmers' market that was held each Tuesday and Thursday in the summer months in Pedeaux. Not wanting anyone to see her, she'd waited until dark, then went to the side of the hotel where the traveling artist had painted the mural years before. She found the door, turned the knob, found it unlocked, and went in. She was smart enough to bring a flashlight. Seeing the stairs, she went up, found the landing, saw the door to the other room, turned the knob, found it unlocked also, and went inside the artist's secret room. It was here she would form the plan to take Mercedes Adler from the hospital and hold her hostage until she would tell them where the Pedosta women had hidden the fortune that was always talked about by the people in town.

Road Trip

Helen's grandmother would tell the little girl stories about the Pedosta fortune and how, after the women had passed away, people would come to Pedeaux to search for the treasure. Most would go away emptyhanded. Others wanted to tear up the house. Some would even go so far as to try to tear the wallpaper from the walls. Her grandmother thought it was awful someone would believe anyone would be so simple as to leave a fortune in the walls of a house.

Before taking Mercedes from the hospital, Helen had cleaned the attic room. She made sure it was free from dust and dirt. When they found Mercedes's body, Helen wanted it noted she was found in a clean room.

It would be so easy to take Mercedes out of the hospital. Helen had a nurse's uniform she had bought at a thrift store for less than two dollars, but a story would have to be devised just in case she was stopped.

Helen found it was very easy to print blank hospital forms off the internet. All one had to do was type into the search engine the key words "hospital forms" and, just like clockwork, blank forms would appear. Helen simply changed the name of the hospital on the form to the one in Pedeaux and she was ready to go.

In her uniform with the fake orders in her hand and pushing a wheelchair, she went into Mercedes's room. There was a female deputy sheriff in the room. Helen showed her the fake orders and explained to Deputy Molly she would be giving Mercedes a pill that was required to be taken before the procedure she was taking Mercedes for. Deputy Molly assisted Helen in placing Mercedes in the wheelchair. Putting her hand out for Deputy Molly to shake, Helen stuck a very small needle into Deputy Molly's hand. It took only a few seconds for Deputy Molly to stop breathing. Helen then dragged Deputy Molly to the linen closet, pushed her inside, locked the door, and left. By the time Helen turned the corner of the hallway, Mercedes was out. Now was the time to find out where the fortune was, get it, get rid of Mercedes, and get out of Pedeaux.

Helen pushed Mercedes out of the hospital into a waiting van. Once she was loaded, Helen ran to her car. Watching as the van pulled away, Helen turned in the opposite direction and made her way to Mercedes's farm to pick up the waiting Sara Nite. By the time she got to the farm, Helen was in a panic. As they say in the movies, "the rest is history." Sara was dead, two sheriff's deputies were dead, and all of this had happened because of Helen Rider.

Well, they'll find out I had the Pedosta brothers killed. They promised me no one would move into the house on the corner. They lied, and you know what happens when someone lies to you, she thought to herself.

Road Trip

Pulling into the parking lot, Helen saw a police car across the street in front of Mercedes's house. As she got out of the car, two policemen walked up to her. Helen just looked at them. The policemen were looking at her license tag, then at her. They asked where she had been, and she proceeded to tell them she had just gotten off work and was going to the hotel to get a bite to eat then go home.

The policemen asked her if they could look in her car. "What for?" she asked. The policemen then explained a car with a woman driving meeting her description was seen leaving the scene of an accident earlier.

Helen looked at the policemen and, as she looked at them, she turned and started to walk away. "Where are you going, miss?" one of the policemen asked.

Helen didn't answer; she just kept walking. The two policemen were stunned to see her just walk away from them. Coming back to their senses, they started after her. When they ordered her to stop, she started walking faster and almost broke into a run. The policemen took off after her. One grabbed her arm and locked it behind her. The other policeman grabbed Helen's other arm, and they cuffed both her hands behind her back.

The policeman who'd caught Helen advised her of her Miranda Rights, and he then put her in the cruiser and headed for the police station.

Chapter 17

When Mercedes woke up, she saw the man who had given her the shot was sleeping on the bed on the other side of the room. Remembering an old television show where someone escaped from zip ties, Mercedes began trying the trick she had seen that showed how someone tied with zip ties could get themselves loose. Moving her feet to the railing of the bed and working the lock of the zip tie back and forth against the railing, she eventually broke the lock of the zip tie, and the restraint came loose. She did the same thing with the zip tie on her other foot.

Reaching down, while keeping an eye on the man on the bed, she removed the ties from her feet, and she stood up. Feeling somewhat wobbly after having been sedated and confined for some time, she looked around for something to tie the man on the bed with. First, she needed to make sure he couldn't get up.

Chapter 17

Spotting a piece of iron that had been part of the headboard, she walked softly over to it and picked it up, but when she turned around, the man was right behind her. He grabbed Mercedes by her hair and pulled her to him. Noticing that all she was wearing was a hospital gown, he tried sticking his hand through her gown. Summoning all the strength she could muster, Mercedes swung the piece of iron around and struck him on the side of his head.

Falling backward, her captor pulled Mercedes on top of him. Struggling to get away, she pushed herself up and moved back toward the wall. Feeling something warm on her hand, she moved quickly to the sunlight streaming in the window. Looking at her hand, she saw it was blood. Turning and looking at the man on the floor, she could see a pool of blood was forming around his head. Walking ever so carefully to the man, she saw his eyes were open as well as his mouth. Reaching down, she felt for a pulse. He was dead.

Mercedes started shaking. Feeling sick, she started to throw up, but nothing was coming out. Becoming dizzy, she fell onto the floor beside the man and passed out.

Chapter 18

Dr. Lajonque, Harper Pedosta, the sheriff, the police chief, and Mercedes sat in the kitchen of the house on the corner.

The kidnapper Mercedes had killed was named Ben Carver. He was a five-time convicted felon with convictions ranging from burglary to attempted murder and was the friend of Sara Nite. As Carver's career in crime had developed, each felony would lead to another, with each felony escalating in violence. It was only just a matter of time before he would have killed Mercedes.

Helen Rider had masterminded the whole plan after she had learned from the Pedosta brothers the possibility of treasure being hidden in the walls of the house on the corner.

Helen's background was much different from Sara's. Both came from dysfunctional homes, only Helen's family had more education and money, none of which was shared with Helen. The women met in prison after both had been

Chapter 18

convicted of felonies ranging from credit card theft and identity theft to grand larceny.

It wasn't hard for Helen to enlist the aid of Ben Carver or the Deputy Gene Lable. Ben would do anything to support his crack cocaine habit, and Gene Lable thought he was in love with Helen Rider.

Mercedes excused herself, telling the group she would be right back. Saying "duty calls," she went upstairs smiling. Moving the bed, she picked up the box that she had put there days earlier.

Going back down the stairs into the kitchen, she handed the box to Harper Pedosta. Harper opened the box, and there before her aging eyes were the bejeweled tap shoes worth more money than Mercedes could imagine. "*Mon amie*, what are you doing?" Harper asked Mercedes.

Mercedes looked at the woman and explained, "These shoes are a part of your family. They belonged to the Pedostas and have caused the death of two of your family members. I am sure the women who had these didn't mean for anyone to die from owning them. I would like to believe they would have converted the jewels in the shoes to money and built the dance studio they so desperately wanted to have."

Harper stood up and walked over and, putting her arms around Mercedes, said, "You have become a part of my family. I will see to it these shoes are put to good use. Even though we cannot build the dance studio, we can at least give part of the money to Al and Aaron's parents. The rest of the money will be used to support the women's shelter. They have been in a bad way for a very long time, and there was talk of closing it. Now, they won't have to, and they can afford to get the kind of people they need in there to help these women."

Epilogue:

Helen Rider was found guilty of kidnapping, one count of manslaughter in the first degree, and two counts of murder for her role in the deaths of Al and Aaron Pedosta. She was sentenced to twenty-five years to life with no chance of parole.

On her way out of the courtroom, she turned to Mercedes and Dr. Lajonque and said, "You think you've seen the last of me? You're wrong. I will get out, and when I do, I will find you. You will pay for what you've done to me."